Agent note happened yesterday.

"I finished in the kitchen about three o'clock," Sharon answered. "We were ready for guests a few minutes before four."

"Just in time to meet Andrew Ballantine."

Sharon hoped that her face didn't reveal her confused emotions—feelings that went counter to her long-held belief that she was much too sensible to fall in love at first sight.

"So, once you began talking with Mr. Ballantine, you lost track of time and the Strathbogie Mist desserts."

"I suppose so."

"Consequently, anyone in the gazebo that afternoon could have tampered with them."

She'd been so engrossed in their conversation that she wouldn't have noticed if a flying saucer had beamed up the ceramic ramekins. But Andrew had declared it "one of the most incredible dishes of Strathbogie Mist I've ever eaten. A dessert to die for."

He doesn't know yet how close he came.

Books by Ron and Janet Benrey

Love Inspired Suspense

Glory Be!
Gone to Glory
Grits and Glory
Season of Glory

*Cozy Mystery

RON AND JANET BENREY

Ron and Janet Benrey began writing romantic cozy mysteries together more than ten years ago—chiefly because they both loved to read them. Their successful collaboration surprised them both, because they have remarkably different backgrounds.

Ron holds degrees in engineering, management and law. He built a successful career as a nonfiction writer specializing in speechwriting and other aspects of business writing. Janet was an entrepreneur before she earned a degree in communications, working in such fields as professional photography, executive recruiting and sporting-goods marketing.

How do they write together and still stay married? That's the question that readers ask most. The answer is that they've developed a process for writing novels that makes optimum use of their individual talents. Perhaps even more important, their love for cozy mysteries transcends the inevitable squabbles when they write one.

Season
OF
Glory

Ron & Janet Benrey

Steeple
Hill®

Published by Steeple Hill Books™

STEEPLE HILL BOOKS

Steeple
Hill®

ISBN-13: 978-0-373-44318-5
ISBN-10:   0-373-44318-8

SEASON OF GLORY

Printed in U.S.A.

My heart took delight in all my work, and this was the reward for all my labor. Yet when I surveyed all that my hands had done and what I had toiled to achieve, everything was meaningless, a chasing after the wind; nothing was gained under the sun.

—*Ecclesiastes* 2:10–11

PROLOGUE

The eighteen guests who attended the Sunday-afternoon tea at The Scottish Captain ate every morsel of food offered to them inside the Captain's back-garden gazebo.

Who could blame them? An authentic Scottish cream tea is not an everyday event in Glory, North Carolina, and the side tables in the gazebo were heaped with handmade sweet scones, clotted cream, twelve kinds of preserves, tea cakes, fruit tartlets, smoked salmon canapés, savory finger sandwiches and dark-chocolate muffins—most prepared by Calvin Constable, the bed-and-breakfast's superb breakfast chef.

The only dish that wasn't Calvin's handiwork was the Strath-bogie Mist, a traditional Scottish concoction of pears, cream, sugar and ginger. Sharon Pickard, the cohostess of the tea party, had made twenty-four helpings, which vanished within seconds of being served.

Sharon had brought the desserts to the gazebo a few minutes before the tea began. "Better leave the ramekins covered for now," Calvin had said to her. "Church elders and committee people can be a ravenous lot."

Sharon laughed, but she felt a twinge of guilt when she saw Emma Neilson scurrying hither and yon in the gazebo—arranging food on tables and putting the final touches on the Christmas decorations. Sharon realized that asking Emma to host a tea party just eleven days before Christmas had added to the chaos of her friend's busy life.

Sharon's own job as head nurse in the emergency room at Glory Regional Hospital could be chock-full of hassles, but Emma, the owner and manager of The Scottish Captain, seemed to work around the clock.

Sharon would have to find a way to repay Emma for her generosity. The hours she'd spent at the Captain hanging Christmas trimmings and helping Calvin in the kitchen were scarcely a down payment.

Thank goodness I never wanted to run a bed-and-breakfast.

"Has the guest of honor arrived yet?" Sharon asked Emma.

"He checked in twenty minutes ago. You'll be surprised when you meet Andrew Ballantine. He seems too young to be an art historian and an expert on stained glass." Emma winked at her. "He's a hunk."

Sharon heard a car door slam in the Captain's parking lot.

"Showtime! The guests are arriving." Emma flipped a switch, turning on the five strings of Christmas lights that ringed the gazebo.

"It'll be beautiful in here when the sun goes down in a few minutes," Sharon said.

"Christmas should be the prettiest time of the year at a B and B."

The partygoers came, welcomed Andrew Ballantine to Glory, ate heartily, drank eight large pots of tea then went home—all without realizing that a serious crime had been committed in their midst.

The senior detective in charge of the criminal investigation was astonished that so many people, gathered together in a small, octagonal summerhouse, had observed so little. After all, two of the merrymakers were members of the Glory Police Department.

Sharon Pickard wasn't the least bit surprised by the general lack of awareness. The invited guests had splintered into six or seven small groups that quickly became lost in conversation. She'd spent most of the party chatting with the guest of honor. They continued to talk long after the gazebo was empty.

Sharon decided that Emma had been right the moment she saw Andrew Ballantine. He looked more like a football player than a consultant who would help Glory Community Church replace a stained-glass window. He was in his midthirties and had an athletic build—she guessed that he stood about six feet, three inches tall and weighed well over two hundred pounds. He wore a heather-colored Harris Tweed jacket and tan slacks that fit him splendidly and went well with his blue eyes and ruddy complexion. His ears were prominent, and his chestnut-colored brown hair was thick enough to flutter in the afternoon breeze. His facial features were craggy rather than classically handsome, but they came together to create a striking whole.

Who cares? Once burned, twice shy.

The familiar maxim was about fire, but it applied equally well to good-looking men. Sharon had learned the hard way that a man's most important feature—his trustworthiness— was invisible from the outside.

Not that Andrew's fidelity made much difference to her. He was a short-term visitor to Glory. They'd spend a few hours working together, and then he'd drive home to Asheville. End of story.

But until he does, there's no reason to be impolite. Or to ignore his positive attributes. Like his smile.

Andrew had a lovely, animated smile, but he never looked happier than when he thanked Sharon for making the Strathbogie Mist.

"It's my all-time favorite Scottish treat," he said.

"I know. I read the article about you in *Church Art Monthly*."

"Every flattering remark is absolutely true."

She grinned. "One thing I don't know—is there a place called Strathbogie?"

He nodded. "It's an area in northeastern Scotland, not far from the modern city of Aberdeen. It's famed for its castle…and obviously for its thick fogs."

He ended his explanation with a curious low-pitched grunt. Sharon might have ignored it, but Andrew immediately made a soft moan, a sound she'd often heard before—from patients in pain. She peered at him. Both the smile and the color were gone from his face.

Oh, my! What's going on?

He grimaced. "I feel dizzy…really dizzy. And my chest hurts." He abruptly tumbled to the floor, smashing a white wicker chair on the way down.

Emma and Calvin were tidying the gazebo. They dropped their trash bags. "I'll call the paramedics," Calvin said.

Emma rolled a tablecloth into a small pillow. "You make him comfortable. I'll try to track down Haley Carroll. She's one of our guests."

Sharon nodded. "The doctor I met here earlier."

She could tell from Andrew's worsening expression that his chest pain had become more intense. "Hang on!" Sharon said. "The paramedics are on their way."

Haley Carroll arrived in less than a minute and checked his vital signs.

"He's seriously ill," she said to Sharon. "It must have been something he ate."

"My food couldn't have hurt him," Calvin said almost pleadingly. "I've been sampling the dishes all day."

Sharon heard Andrew begin to retch. And then the implications of what Calvin had said hit home. It must have been her Strathbogie Mist that had made Andrew ill.

No! That's not possible.

She saw red flashing lights above the fence that separated the parking lot from the garden. *An ambulance.* She moved closer to Andrew and knelt down. *Save the explanations for later. All that matters now is keeping him alive.*

ONE

Sharon Pickard stepped past the unhung Christmas decorations lying on the floor of the nurses' lounge and hoped that the joy of the season would rub off on the dour-faced detective who'd shown up at the emergency room and asked to see her. He was wide and muscular and had a shaven head. But most formidable of all were his probing black eyes that made it difficult for Sharon to maintain a friendly smile on her own face. Well, intimidating or not, she had no choice but to speak to the police this afternoon. Someone had committed a serious crime yesterday, and she was partly involved.

At least, around the edges.

She pushed a cardboard box full of Christmas tree ornaments sideways on an old vinyl upholstered sofa to make room for the big man, and then read the business card he had handed her. *Special Agent Tyrone C. Keefe, North Carolina State Bureau of Investigation.*

"We'll have to keep this discussion brief, Agent Keefe." She sat down on the top step of a stubby wooden stepladder that someone had used to hang decorations on the artificial Christmas tree in the corner. "I go back on duty at one o'clock. We'll have the lounge to ourselves until then. The other off-duty nurses are at lunch."

He scowled at his watch. "I'm investigating an attempted murder, Ms. Pickard. Twenty minutes may not be enough time for you to answer all of my questions." His skeptical tone seemed to demand a more detailed explanation from her.

"Glory, North Carolina is a small town," she said quickly, "and Glory Regional Hospital has limited resources. I'm the only nurse on staff with hands-on experience treating acute cardio-glycoside poisoning."

"Really?" His dark eyes zeroed in on her. "How did you acquire your expertise, Ms. Pickard?"

She grasped her mistake at once. Her offhand remark revealed that she had the specific know-how to kill people with oleander.

Now he'll consider me the prime suspect.

Her heart began to thud. She felt uneasy—much like when a police car appeared in her rearview mirror then zipped past her on the highway.

The last thing a nurse needs is a reputation as a poisoner.

"Ten years ago I took part in a three-month medical mission to Sri Lanka, the island nation in the Indian Ocean that used to be called Ceylon."

He gave a quick nod. "Go on."

"I worked in a rural hospital that routinely treated people for oleander poisoning. Chewing oleander seeds is a popular way to commit suicide in Sri Lanka."

"Is that what happened to Andrew Ballantine at the tea party? Did someone feed him a handful of oleander seeds?"

"Probably not. Every part of an oleander plant is full of heart-stopping toxin. It's simple to make a lethal infusion by soaking leaves, stems or seeds in boiling water."

"And I suppose it would have been equally *simple* for someone to add a few spoonfuls of oleander broth to the unusual dessert Mr. Ballantine ate yesterday afternoon at The Scottish Captain." He made an indistinct gesture. "I forget its name."

"Strathbogie Mist," she said. "Crushed pears topped with ginger-flavored whipped cream. Served chilled, of course."

"Of course." He smirked wryly. "We're fairly certain that the Strathbogie Mist you served Mr. Ballantine contained the poison he ingested. We'll be entirely certain when our forensic laboratory finishes testing the…ah, *ramekins* that held the dessert. However, your pear concoction appears to be the only item he ate that came in an individual serving."

His high-powered gaze impelled her to turn away. It was probably a technique he'd perfected over the years to encourage people to tell him the truth. She focused for a while on the battered Coke machine in the corner and prayed he didn't sense her blood beginning to boil. How dare he even suggest that she'd poisoned Andrew?

"For your information, Agent Keefe," she retorted, "I didn't *serve* Andrew Ballantine anything. The helpings of Strathbogie Mist were set out on a buffet table—in The Scottish Captain's backyard gazebo."

"And you know that because…?"

"I put them on the table." She looked Agent Keefe directly in the eyes to convince him she was telling the truth. "I made the dessert yesterday, a few hours before the tea party began. I crushed the pears, I whipped the cream, I even filled the ramekins." She took a quick breath. "But despite your heavy-handed insinuation, I didn't lace Andrew's portion with oleandrin."

"What's oleandrin?"

"The poisonous toxin in oleander—the cardiac glycoside that nearly switched off his heart."

Agent Keefe smirked again. "You think I'm heavy-handed, Ms. Pickard? Look at the crime from my vantage point. You had the best opportunity to poison Mr. Ballantine, along with easy access to the toxin. There's an oleander bush in the Captain's back garden, less than twenty feet away from the kitchen door."

Sharon murmured a silent thank-you that Emma Neilson, the owner of The Scottish Captain, had married Glory's Deputy Chief of Police. Early that Monday morning, Rafe Neilson had telephoned Sharon to explain that he'd requested assistance from the North Carolina State Bureau of Investigation. "I had no choice," he'd said. "It would be highly inappropriate for me to investigate an intentional poisoning at my wife's B and B."

Rafe had continued. "The NCSBI is sending Ty Keefe to conduct the interviews. He's smart, experienced and an expert at spotting evasion, so be totally open with him. Don't even think about lying."

With Rafe's safe advice fresh in her mind, Sharon took a moment to frame a response to Agent Keefe's near-accusation. "Why would I want to poison Andrew Ballantine? He was a complete stranger to me when he walked into the gazebo. He lives in Asheville, on the other side of North Carolina."

"I was going to ask you about that." Keefe gazed at her once again with an intensity she could almost feel. "Two other people who went to the tea party told me that you latched on to Mr. Ballantine like he was an old friend—that you barely spoke with anyone else."

Sharon felt herself blush. "At first we talked about Glory Community Church. He'd spent two hours on Sunday afternoon inside the sanctuary looking at the stained-glass windows. He had several questions about the church and Pastor Hartman. After I answered them, we discussed our shared interests, like Scotland and the Scots. The time flew by."

"Until he collapsed in a heap."

She nodded. "Oleandrin often triggers bradycardia, a dangerously low pulse rate. Andrew became pale, said he was feeling nauseated, and then fainted. I called the paramedics. Emma Neilson folded a tablecloth into a makeshift pillow to help make Andrew comfortable. One of the guests at the B and B— Haley Carroll, a physician—worked on him until the ambulance arrived."

"And once at the hospital Mr. Ballantine received some kind of high-tech antidote?"

Sharon answered with an ambiguous shrug. Agent Keefe must've known that she couldn't voluntarily provide specific details about Andrew's treatment to the police, although there wasn't much to keep private. Andrew's overnight stay in the E.R. was a simple tale with a happy ending. The "high-tech antidote" for oleandrin poisoning was antidigoxin antibodies— a therapy originally developed to treat digitalis overdoses. Five vials helicoptered to Glory from Duke Medical Center in Durham had worked well for Andrew.

Ken Lehman, the lead emergency room physician at Glory Regional had also followed the "old fashioned" treatment protocol throughout the night: He encouraged Andrew to throw up, treated his various cardiac symptoms as they appeared, and gave him multiple doses of activated charcoal to absorb the oleandrin left in his system.

Agent Keefe retrieved a small notebook from his jacket pocket. "Tell me what happened yesterday from the beginning—

when you arrived at The Scottish Captain. I'm curious why an emergency room nurse would spend her day off cooking a Scottish dessert in a local B and B."

"Two months ago an electrical fire in the sanctuary of Glory Community Church destroyed one of the church's stained-glass windows," Sharon explained. "The Window Restoration Committee was organized to oversee the window's replacement. I'm the Chair of the WinReC, as we've come to be called."

"And the members decided to hire Andrew Ballantine to act as your stained-glass window guru," Keefe interrupted. "I interviewed Emma Neilson this morning. I know that she's also a member of the committee and that she agreed to host a welcoming tea party for Mr. Ballantine in the Captain's garden gazebo." He leaned against the sofa. "Let's get back to you."

"I offered to pitch in because Emma is the best friend I have in Glory."

Sharon peered sideways at Agent Keefe. He seemed to accept her statement without any questions. Good. She didn't want to have to explain the details of her friendship with Emma to the nosy detective.

They'd met the previous March when Sharon, who sang alto, had joined the choir at Glory Community Church. Emma, a soprano, had recently returned from her honeymoon with Rafe. Sharon and Emma quickly discovered the many other things in addition to good voices they had in common—from a love of women's softball, to a dislike of church politics, to the painful fact that both had moved to Glory from big cities to escape the stress of messy divorces from unfaithful men.

Stress was the key word. Shedding her husband of six years, starting a new job and moving from Raleigh to Glory had filled her days with "stress points" a year earlier. Blessedly, her new

life in Glory now seemed more or less normal—but here was
Agent Keefe, trying his best to crank up the pressure.

He would never understand, but filling her free Sunday with
busy work had been a fair trade. Helping out in the Captain's
kitchen had benefited Emma. But equally important, enjoying
a productive Sunday with a friend at The Scottish Captain had
softened the reality that she would go through another Christmas season alone.

"Anyway," Sharon said, "I arrived at the Captain at one
o'clock and began making the Strathbogie Mist. I also worked
with Calvin Constable, the Captain's breakfast chef, to prepare
the scones and tea cakes."

"In other words, you spent the afternoon in the kitchen?"

She thought about this. "Except for two ten-minute breaks
when I helped Emma greet arriving guests, starting with the
Dickensons—a couple from Pennsylvania. She's a dentist,
he's a lawyer."

Sharon wondered if she should share her other routine
observations—that Samuel and Theodora Dickenson were a
well-tanned, healthy-looking duo: she a lean woman with
caramel-colored hair; he somewhat chubbier with ashen hair
and a trim brown goatee.

*No need. Agent Keefe undoubtedly spoke to them this
morning, too.*

"Next, I met the Carrolls, from Wilson, North Carolina," she
said. Haley Carroll—an anesthesiologist—was a round-faced
redhead, while Michael Carroll—an accountant—was a rangy,
mostly nondescript man with an unusually large nose.

Agent Keefe flipped a page in his notebook. "One other
guest arrived on Sunday afternoon. A Mrs. Amanda Turner."

"She checked in while I was cooking. Emma showed her through the kitchen when I was putting away the mixing bowls I'd used." Sharon recalled that Emma hadn't looked especially happy when she led the fortyish, full-figured woman with brassy blond hair through the kitchen's swinging door.

"This is Amanda Turner," Emma had said with a noticeably strained smile. "Amanda hails from Birmingham, Alabama. She recently purchased The Robert Burns Inn, the B and B on Campbell Street. She's staying with us until the painters and carpet layers finish redecorating the guest rooms."

"They promised to be done by Wednesday," Amanda drawled, "but I almost don't care, because I know I'm going to enjoy my stay here. The Captain is so lovely, and now I have a chance to see every last inch of the building."

Sharon had instantly understood Emma's hesitation. She wasn't thrilled to give a future competitor a comprehensive tour of The Scottish Captain, but she could hardly refuse, because Amanda was a legitimate paying customer.

Agent Keefe clicked his ballpoint pen then jotted a few words. "How many portions of Strathbogie Mist did you make for the tea party?"

"Twenty-four."

"All identical?"

"Completely. I filled two dozen six-ounce ceramic ramekins."

"When did you finish?"

"About three o'clock."

Keefe made a noncommittal grunt. "What were you wearing when you prepared the dessert?"

The sudden shift in topic startled Sharon. "I beg your pardon. What difference does my clothing make?"

"You wore some sort of pants suit to the tea party. I doubt

you worked in the kitchen dressed like that. Where did you leave the puddings when you went home to change?"

She fought back a snicker. "Some sort of pants suit" was made of dark green Dupioni silk, had cost the better part of a month's salary, and accentuated the best aspects of her figure. It was her Christmas gift to herself this year. She'd seen it at the Glorious Boutique on Main Street and had straight away given in to temptation. Well, why even try to resist? She had no one in her life to buy expensive presents for—and no one to buy them for her.

And no one to tell me blatant lies about business meetings that take all evening...

"Actually, Agent Keefe, I dressed for the tea party in Emma and Rafe Neilson's bedroom—but I see where you're going. In fact, the ramekins were never left alone during the afternoon. You can check with Calvin Constable, but I believe he kept working in the kitchen when I went upstairs to change."

"I did check with Mr. Constable," Keefe confirmed. "When did you move the desserts to the gazebo?"

"About a quarter to four. Calvin and I used a kitchen cart to wheel all the goodies from the kitchen through the garden. We took turns carrying dishes up the gazebo's front steps. We were ready for guests a few minutes before four."

"Just in time for you to meet Andrew Ballantine."

Sharon hoped that her face didn't reveal her confused emotions. Everything had happened so quickly and she had spent most of the night in the emergency room doing what was necessary to keep him alive. She and Ken Lehman had worked together in an E.R. resuscitation bay, equipped with patient monitors and a defibrillator in the event they had to restart Andrew's heart.

Sometime during the evening her own heart had restarted. She realized that she no longer saw him as a "consultant" or even as a "patient." And to her great surprise she'd stopped worrying about Andrew's trustworthiness. He'd made a wondrous first impression on her, although she wasn't sure how he managed to do it. She had prayed during every step of the treatment they'd administered, surprised at the depth of her affection for Andrew that had intensified as she worked to maintain his steady heartbeat. She'd reminded herself over and over again that she'd met him the previous afternoon, that they'd spoken for only an hour, that she knew almost nothing about his personal life—other than he'd grown up in Knoxville, Tennessee, traveled far and wide to do his job, and saw himself as a confirmed bachelor. But biographic details seemed less important than the chief thing she didn't know—how Andrew felt about her.

Stop acting like a harebrained sixteen-year-old. You're on the verge of making a fool of yourself.

But logic was ineffective against those pesky feelings she felt—feelings that countered her long-held belief that she was much too sensible a person to fall in love at first sight.

At the party, she'd had to remind herself to stop gaping at the man—and to stop thinking of Andrew Ballantine as perfect. Even now, the memories of that opening hour with Andrew made it difficult to concentrate on Agent Keefe's ardent questions.

Keefe went on. "So, once you began talking with Mr. Ballantine, you lost track of time and the Strathbogie Mist."

"I suppose so."

"Consequently, anyone in the gazebo that afternoon could have tampered with the desserts."

"True enough." Sharon thought back to the tea party. The gazebo had appeared crowded, what with the Dickensons, the

Carrolls and Amanda Turner talking together and various members of the church coming and going. Sharon supposed that there must have been a dozen people milling about, greeting Rafe and Emma Neilson, and saying hello to Andrew.

She and Andrew eventually moved to a quiet spot two steps down the wide staircase. She'd been so engrossed in their conversation that she wouldn't have noticed if a flying saucer had beamed up the ceramic ramekins—at least not until Andrew had decided to try one of her homemade treats. He had declared it "one of the most incredible dishes of Strathbogie Mist I've ever eaten. Better than my grandmother's. A dessert to die for."

He doesn't know yet how close he came.

"Unfortunately," Keefe said, "that leaves us with an open-ended array of potential suspects, unless…" He smiled crookedly. "Unless I can find solid evidence that you did it."

Sharon let herself frown. "You seem to have forgotten that I cared for Andrew most of last night. If I wanted to kill him, I had plenty of good opportunities when he was unconscious in the emergency room."

"Not necessarily. You knew by then that you'd be considered a suspect in his poisoning. Killing him in the E.R. would have involved too much risk. No—we can be confident that Mr. Ballantine was safe in your hands last night."

"And he'll be safe in my hands today," she murmured.

"Did you say something?" He stood up and pointed at the clock over the door. "Look at that—we finished a full minute ahead of time."

"I said that you aren't very bright if you seriously think that I poisoned Andrew Ballantine."

He shrugged. "At this point in my investigation, everyone who attended the tea party is a person of interest. But I'll admit that you're pretty low on my list of suspects. What's more, I'm rooting that you *didn't* do it. Good E.R. nurses are in short supply these days and Rafe Neilson told me that you are considered one of the best in the Carolinas."

He pulled open the heavy metal door that led to the hospital's main corridor. He waited until he stood on the threshold to continue. "However, the fact remains that someone tried to kill Mr. Ballantine—someone with a motive we don't understand. I'd like to close the case before the perpetrator strikes again."

Sharon smothered a gasp. The notion of a repeat attack hadn't occurred to her. Was someone in Glory determined to kill Andrew Ballantine? And would that person try again?

TWO

How do I get them to tell me the whole truth?

Andrew Ballantine mulled over his situation and cataloged the six forlorn facts he knew for certain:

1. According to the embroidered label on his blanket, he was a "guest" of Glory Regional Hospital.

2. He'd spent an entire night in a hospital for the first time in his life.

3. He'd been asleep much of that night—drifting in and out of consciousness.

4. He'd awoken at 10:00 a.m. and now felt reasonably clear-headed, although his innards still ached a bit.

5. His illness, whatever its cause, had begun at an afternoon tea party—he dimly recollected drinking a mug of an especially fine Indian Assam.

6. The nurse who'd visited him twice to take his temperature this morning—a rosy cheeked woman named Melanie, who looked about twelve years old—repeatedly replied "I don't know" when he asked what was wrong with him or why he was attached to five different medical monitors.

Andrew lifted the blanket and peered at the various wires

connected to circular pads stuck on his chest, arms and legs, and contemplated yanking the clips loose.

"That would set off the alarms and start a noisy commotion," he mused. "Maybe then someone in this hospital will tell me what's going on."

A tap on the door interrupted his scheming. "Mr. Ballantine?"

Now what? It seemed too soon for another visit from Melanie. Besides, she didn't knock; she simply stormed in.

"Come in," he said.

The door opened, revealing a strikingly attractive woman wearing sky-blue scrubs. It took him a few seconds to recognize her as the woman he'd talked with for more than an hour at the tea party. Sharon…

Rats! I've forgotten her last name.

She smiled at him from the doorway. "How do you feel?"

"Confused. No one will tell me what put me in a hospital. I woke up an hour ago, and I've received a full-blown runaround since then."

"That's my fault, I'm afraid." She moved into the room. "None of the staff who came on duty after seven o'clock this morning knows the whole story of why you're here. I haven't had a chance to bring the nurses up to speed."

Andrew struggled to think of Sharon's last name. She'd looked different in The Scottish Captain's back garden. Her complexion had seemed more golden in the late afternoon sun, especially in contrast to the deep green of her outfit. But her blue scrubs this morning and the cool fluorescent overhead lighting in his room conspired to made her skin look pale, almost porcelainlike.

Yesterday, her ash blond hair had brushed her shoulders; now, it was tightly pinned back. One feature hadn't changed, however. Despite her metal-rimmed glasses, her amber eyes appeared as luminous as when he'd stood next to her on the gazebo steps—and even more lively.

A vision flashed in Andrew's mind. "I remember a stocky man," he said. "In his forties. Mostly bald with a friendly face and a small goatee. He kept shining a light in my eyes."

"Ken Lehman is our lead emergency room physician. He spent most of the night working on you."

"I want to talk to Dr. Lehman. How can I get hold of him?"

"You can't right now. He went home to get some sleep."

"He's home sleeping? That's just wonderful!"

"Actually, it is wonderful," she said. "I had to fight with Ken to make him leave the E.R. He came on duty at two o'clock. yesterday afternoon, and it wasn't until five this morning that he agreed you'd made sufficient enough progress for him to get some rest. I promised to monitor you and call him if your condition gets worse."

"Will I get worse?"

"No. You're on the mend."

Another memory jogged his mind. He'd woken up briefly during the night and seen a patchwork of images: a tress of blond hair, a woman praying silently and the glint of a needle attached to a green plastic tube.

"You were my nurse last night, right? You stuck something in my arm."

Her amber eyes flashed mischievously. "Several somethings."

Concentrate! What's her last name?

Andrew tried to dredge up their conversation in the gazebo. Had she told him that she was an emergency room nurse? Probably, and many other things about herself, too—but most of the tea party was still a blank in his mind.

You're not as clearheaded as you thought you were.

He peered at her nametag, but her last name was too small to decipher from across the room.

"On the mend from what?" he asked.

She took a step toward him. "You were poisoned."

"Tainted food! I thought it must be something like that." He shook his head in mock sadness. "That's what happens when Americans attempt to cook Scottish vittles without proper training. No doubt a fusty scone I ate at afternoon tea *laid me loo*—as my Scottish grandmother would say."

He expected her to nod, but surprisingly her face darkened. "None of the food you ate at the party made you ill." Then she glared at him. "Not even the dessert I prepared."

Embarrassment tore through him. "I remember. You made the Strathbogie Mist."

"Which you loved."

"How could I not? It's comfort food straight from my childhood. My grandmother served us Strathbogie Mist every Sunday—even during the winter when she used canned pears instead of fresh. That's why I ate two helpings at the tea party."

"Now you're fibbing," she said with a laugh. "There weren't any extra portions."

She came another step closer. At last, he could read her nametag.

Pickard. Sharon Pickard!

"There must have been extras," he said. "Two of those little ceramic dishes appeared by my side. I don't recall who gave me the first one, but I'm all but certain that Emma Neilson brought me the second helping a few minutes later."

Her smile vanished. "I wish you hadn't eaten any." She sat down in the visitor's chair alongside his bed and pointed at his heart. "You were poisoned. *Really* poisoned. Someone tried to kill you by spiking one of your ramekins with oleander toxin. You consumed more than enough toxin to stop your heart. Oleander poisoning has a high death rate. You could easily have died last night."

Andrew glanced at her fingers a few inches from his chest, and then at the anxious grimace on her face. All at once, the words she spoke hit home. *Poisoned. Toxin. Stop your heart. Death.* He shivered as he recognized that she sincerely meant everything she said. He made a feeble wave toward the medical monitors in the room. "All these electronic gadgets…you actually used this stuff on me?"

"Every last screen, meter and dial."

"I could have died…" he said without meaning to.

"But you didn't. Ken Lehman kept you alive."

Andrew recalled that he'd seen many glimpses of blond hair during the night. "Ken and *you*."

"True. I helped Ken," she replied with a new smile that made her face glow.

He realized that he was gawking at Sharon. Her jubilant expression made her more than striking—she'd become beautiful.

Stare at her later. After she's answered all your questions.

"You said that the toxin I downed came from oleander. Do you mean the shrubby evergreen with large five-petalled blossoms? The plant some people call rosebay?"

She nodded. "Is gardening one of your hobbies?"

"I'm not sure I could recognize an oleander in the flesh, so to speak, but during the 19th century, the Ballantine Studios built several church windows that incorporate oleanders in their designs. I'm quite familiar with the stained-glass rendering of the plant. Some have pink blossoms, others white."

"Oleander is an efficient killer. Fortunately, the symptoms

you presented helped Ken Lehman make a quick diagnosis. You even had the classic redness of the skin around your mouth." She touched the depression on his face, just above his chin. "It hasn't faded yet."

Andrew shivered at her touch, astonished at its gentleness. He thought back to the tea party. He remembered feeling woozy, uncoordinated. He wondered what he'd eaten that was making him nauseated and his insides ache. Then he became dizzy and everything changed perspective. He slowly became aware that he'd tumbled to the floor. His side hurt, but nowhere near as much as his stomach. He'd probably hit something solid, perhaps a chair, on his way down.

Someone was shaking his shoulder. He opened his eyes and saw Sharon.

"Dr. Carroll," she said. "Can you take a look at Andrew?"

A moment later, Andrew felt a woman's fingers touch his wrist and then the artery in his neck.

"His pupils are dilated and I don't like his pulse. I barely felt anything in his wrist and his carotid pulse isn't much stronger. I wish I had my medical bag."

"I know that Emma has an EpiPen auto-injector inside the Captain's first-aid kit," Sharon said. "Could this be some kind of allergic reaction?"

"I doubt it. He doesn't have the other symptoms of allergic shock."

"Hang on, Andrew," Sharon said. "The paramedics are on their way."

"Praise God for that," Andrew had muttered. The pain in his stomach had become sharper, more concentrated. And then his chest had felt tight. He could tell that something was wrong with his heart. Could he be having a heart attack?

Not when I'm only thirty-four years old.

Emma had said, "Here's a folded tablecloth. I'm going to put in under your head."

"What a good idea," Andrew had replied, softly. Despite the aches in his stomach and his chest, he'd begun to feel drowsy. Why not take a little nap? He'd had a long day, starting with a seven-hour drive from Asheville…then he'd studied the church windows…and then all the talking at the tea party…

Returning to the present, Andrew found the bed remote control and worked the button that lifted him to a sitting position. "I don't even remember the trip in the ambulance."

"You were unconscious when we strapped you to the gurney." Sharon's face was filled with anxiety again. "Oleander toxin causes a variety of heart rhythm problems—all of them serious."

He tried to assess the beating of his heart. The gentle throb inside him seemed normal, although something Sharon had said kept nudging at his thoughts.

"Look…I don't have any enemies in Glory—or in Asheville, for that matter. I can't get my head around the idea that someone poisoned me on purpose."

"The police confirmed it."

"*The police?* So it's an official investigation?"

"That's right. They consider your poisoning attempted murder." She tossed her head unhappily. "In fact, a special agent named Keefe wants to talk to you. I told him you'd be ready to be interviewed later this afternoon."

"Sheesh!"

"And a dozen reporters have called the hospital asking about you. By evening, your story will be front-page news from coast to coast." She looked faintly amused. "Who can blame them? It's not often that a famous stained-glass guru is poisoned by a toxic Scottish dessert during afternoon tea at a small-town bed-and-breakfast."

"Whoa! Who says I'm famous?"

"The Internet." She held up a wireless laptop computer. "Last night while I was waiting for the antitoxin we gave you to do its thing, I accessed a search engine and entered your name."

"Don't believe everything you find on the Net."

"I discovered that Glory Community Church imported *the* world's foremost expert on painted stained-glass windows. We knew that you're the great-great-great-grandson of James Ballantine of Edinburgh, the man who built our windows. But we didn't know that you're celebrated on four continents."

"In highly limited circles." He let himself grin. "But world expert or not, I have no interest in talking to reporters."

"Bless you! The Scottish Captain doesn't deserve a flood of negative publicity merely because Emma Neilson did a good deed and hosted a tea party."

"Talking about good deeds…I need to get back to work. I have a presentation to prepare. I'm scheduled to speak to the elders of the Church tomorrow evening." He laughed. "Well, you know that. You sent me the invitation."

"If you take it easy today," she said, "I'll do my best to get you released tomorrow."

"I'm feeling fine."

"You look fine, too. But five hours ago, you were sleeping in our emergency room—and twelve hours ago, we had you listed in critical condition."

"And so, I'm stuck here in bed until tomorrow morning?"

"Until we're sure that your heart rhythm is back to normal." She swung her index finger to and fro like a metronome. "I'll keep you company for a while."

Andrew saw something blossom in Sharon's eyes that he tried to gauge. Was it…*enthusiasm?* Did she enjoy spending time with him? He felt a ripple of concern. He'd never been good at reading women's faces. Her "enthusiasm" might be nothing more than wishful thinking on his part, or maybe her routine attempt to come across as polite and professional.

They had spoken for a long time at the tea party. He must have liked her then…he certainly liked her now. But what had they talked about? He remembered only snips and scraps of their conversation. They were both single. They both enjoyed skiing. And both bicycled from their homes to their workplaces. Not much to go on. Worst of all, he didn't recall her body language or the other non-verbal cues that signaled her thoughts about him.

"What else did you learn about me on the Internet?"

Andrew squirmed at the clumsiness of his own words. *You sound like an egotistical clod.* Ask about her.

Before he could undo the damage, she said, "I learned that we have something in common."

She reached into her pocket and brought out a cell phone that was also a personal-digital assistant. She pressed a few buttons. A photograph of a small white dog appeared on the screen.

"Meet Heather Pickard."

"You have a Scottish Terrier, too?"

"Heather is three years old. She isn't a show dog, like your Scottie."

"You've heard about MacTavish? Well, he's retired from the show ring." He looked around for the telephone. "I have dozens of photos in my laptop. If I can get someone to retrieve it from the Captain, I'll dazzle you with Mac's portfolio."

Sharon pulled a face. "Nice try. But no laptops or cell phones until tomorrow. You'll have to make do with conversation today."

"In that case, let me ask you a question. You know how to cook Scottish desserts, you have a Scottish Terrier, and you live in Glory, North Carolina, a town founded by Scots. I see a pattern developing. Am I right?"

"It's true that I like Scottish things…" She smiled then added, "All except plaid."

"Me, too—but I can explain my Scotophilia. It's in my blood. What's your excuse?"

She began to laugh. "You used the wrong word. *Scotophilia* is a medical term that means a preference for darkness or night. You don't seem the type of person who avoids the light."

"Scotophilia is also a fondness for Scotland and the Scots. I found the definition on the Internet."

She laughed louder.

"Anyway," he said. I'm a *Scotophile* because my grand-parents moved from Scotland to North Carolina after WWII."

She stopped laughing long enough to say, "As a matter of fact, so did my grandparents. The Pickards hail from Glasgow."

"I can't believe that Pickard is a Scottish name. It sounds French."

"Our Scottish branch isn't as large as the Ballantine Clan, but 'men of Picardy' have lived in Scotland for hundreds of years."

Andrew forced himself to look at the small Christmas wreath on the wall above Sharon's head and count the four gold angels and nine silvery stars. From what he'd seen, the hospital had been restrained in putting up Christmas decorations. Still, thanks to the holiday season, he could gaze at something other than Sharon's lovely face.

Don't say what you want to say.

He ached to tell Sharon that that she looked her most lovely when she laughed—but that would probably make her laugh *at him*. Even if it didn't, why start something that would only lead to disappointment. Some guys weren't meant for long-term relationships. *You, for example. You've proven that enough times to recognize the truth.*

Help them restore the church window, and then get out of Glory.

THREE

Sharon waited in the hospital's lobby, her mind filled with the hazy notion that she was about to lead Andrew Ballantine into harm's way. As the patient in Room 204, he was relatively safe—especially with the formidable Special Agent Keefe still poking around, annoying the E.R. staff and paramedics with questions. But outside the hospital—well, anything could happen in the real world.

She watched the elevator door slide open. Melanie Luft, the floor-duty nurse who'd cared for Andrew, pushed his wheelchair alongside the Information kiosk in the lobby.

Melanie looked elfin in a Santa hat as she walked back to the elevator—a reminder that Christmas was only nine days away. But despite the approaching holiday, Sharon found the hat more frivolous than festive. The thought of a poisoner stalking Andrew had overwhelmed the joy of the season. It no longer felt like Christmas to Sharon.

Her former husband had announced his intention to leave a few days before Christmas two years ago. She'd urged herself not to allow the divorce to destroy her love of Christmas—and she'd succeeded. But how could she enjoy the Season of Lights this year when Andrew might be in lethal peril?

Andrew waved at her, a cheerful smile on his face. She jogged to the wheelchair and reprimanded him, "Let's get one thing straight. You're not going to overexert yourself today."

"Wow! Did I do something wrong?"

Sharon winced at her overreaction to his understandable pleasure at leaving the hospital. She'd scolded Andrew, she knew, because she was worried about him—and also harbored guilt for orchestrating his premature release.

"Your cardiologist wanted you to spend another day in bed until we're entirely sure your heart rhythm is back to normal," she said briskly. "I talked her into letting you go this morning— with the understanding that you'd have a no-stress day and wear a real-time cardiac monitor."

Andrew patted the book-sized plastic box clipped to his belt. "Melanie described it as a portable patient monitor."

"It's more than that. There's a cell phone module inside that transmits your cardiac data back to the hospital every hour. It will report abnormal rhythms as soon as they occur."

He peered up at her. "I just noticed…you're not wearing scrubs."

The admiration she could hear in his voice pleased her. She'd chosen her simple outfit—a cashmere sweater and designer jeans—because it flattered her figure. This wasn't a date, but why not look her best?

"I'm your chauffeuse today," she said. "You're not allowed to drive until you rack up twenty-four more hours of normal heartbeats, so I arranged for another nurse to replace me in the E.R." She stepped behind Andrew, took hold of the wheelchair's handles, and pushed the chair toward the hallway that led to the parking garage.

"Thanks for springing me from Glory Regional. Another

night upstairs would have driven me bonkers." He added, "I'm raring to get to work."

"Don't 'rare' too hard. You'll trigger your cardiac surveillance system."

"I feel fine." He glanced at her over his shoulder. "Admit it— I even look healthy."

She replied by pushing the wheelchair faster. It was true that Andrew seemed as hale and hardy as when she first saw him. But she knew that Sharon Pickard, Committee Chair, *not* Sharon Pickard, Registered Nurse, had championed Andrew's early "parole" from medical care—for purely practical reasons.

Andrew was scheduled to speak at a special Tuesday night elders' meeting at Glory Community Church, where he would present for their approval his recommended strategy for restoring the broken stained-glass window. Alas, it was too close to Christmas to reschedule the meeting. If Andrew didn't speak tonight, the committee work she found so tedious would drag on another month.

Well, whatever her motives for persuading his cardiologist, Andrew would remain "fine" and "healthy" today. She'd be at his side throughout the day—his own private duty nurse.

I won't let him overdo. And I'll make sure he's not poisoned again.

She paused in front of the sensor to allow the electric doors to open, then pushed the wheelchair into the parking garage.

"I can walk from here," Andrew said.

"Stay put! My car is at the other end. I intend to bring the wheelchair with us today. In case we need it."

"I feel silly being wheeled around."

"Get used to it. It's all part of the deal I made."

"Whew! You can be tough," he said with a chuckle.

"Not tough enough," she murmured. *I didn't say no to Pastor Hartman.*

Daniel Hartman had approached her just before Thanksgiving. "Sharon, we need someone like you to chair our Window Restoration Committee."

"I'm not a committee person," she'd said truthfully. "I'm impatient and not at all diplomatic."

Daniel countered her objections. "It'll be an easy job for someone with your organizational skills and experience. It's a small committee—only three members plus yourself. You'll meet occasionally to decide the best way to repair our damaged stained-glass window. Once the committee recommends a course of action to the elders, Ann Trask Miller—our church administrator—will oversee the actual construction work when the restoration strategy is approved by the elders."

He'd made it seem like such a simple assignment. But the "occasional meetings" had quickly become three meetings a week as the WinReC discovered that the job of restoring a stained-glass window was a festival of unforeseen complexities. After two weeks of wheel-spinning, the members reluctantly decided to import a stained-glass expert to help them plan a restoration strategy.

"End of the line. Here's my car." She stopped in front of a compact sedan. "You buckle up in the passenger seat while I collapse the wheelchair and stow it in the trunk."

"Where are you taking me?"

"To your office."

"I have an office?"

"We didn't get the chance to tell you on Sunday, but Gordie Pollack set up an office for you to use while you're in Glory."

"Did I meet Gordie at the tea party?"

"Briefly. He's the Director of the Scottish Heritage Society, Glory's Number-One expert on our Scottish traditions and history. He's also a member of the church's Window Restoration Committee. He's become the project's "historic conscience"—the person who champions the window's cultural significance."

Sharon climbed into the driver's seat and started the engine.

"Glory is a small town," Andrew said, "and it's a fine morning for a brisk stroll. Do we really have to drive to my office?"

"True. I agree. And, yes—it's not negotiable." She put the car in gear. "No brisk strolls until your cardiologist feels confident you won't suffer another bout of bradycardia."

"I'll say it again. You're tough."

She drove in silence for more than a minute. "That impressive stone and granite edifice ahead on the left, on the corner of Front and Main, is the Glory National Bank Building—the tallest structure in Glory."

"Our destination?"

"Yep. Your office is on the second floor."

Sharon found a parking space in front of the building.

"What happens now?" Andrew said.

"We'll risk you walking from here on."

Sharon followed Andrew into the building then through the high-ceilinged lobby, her heels tapping on the marble floor.

"Let's climb the staircase to the second floor," he said.

"Let's not. A sudden increase in your pulse might trigger your heart monitor. If that happens, we'd be hip deep in paramedics."

Sharon noted that Andrew stared straight ahead as they rode up in the elevator. He must've been getting irritated with her seemingly foolish edicts. Well, the world would be back to normal tomorrow—for him and for her.

The Scottish Heritage Society occupied a small suite on the eastern end of the second floor. Gordie Pollack gave Sharon a hug, then moved toward Andrew, his hand outstretched. "The last time I saw you, Andrew," he said, "you were as dark green as a MacAulay hunting tartan. I'm delighted to see you returned to the pink."

He trilled his tongue as he said "dark" and "returned," combining his mellifluous voice with a thick Scots accent to create a sound that Sharon found delightful. Gordie was charming and friendly, with bright blue eyes and handsome features. The ladies in Glory loved him, but he was firmly attached to Siobhan Pollock—who was as proud of her Irish ancestry as he was of his Scottish.

Sharon smiled as Andrew took up the Scottish brogue challenge. "Aye, Mr. Pollack," he said. "I only wish everyone in Glory was as perceptive as ye. The doctors at the hospital fear I'm still ailing and as helpless as a wee bairn."

"Enough Scottish games," she chided. "Let's put Andrew to work."

"Certainly…" Andrew said with the longest trill of all.

"I yield to your rolling of the Rs." Gordie raised his hands in mock surrender. "I converted our conference room into a guest office for you. We retrieved your laptop bag this morning from The Scottish Captain, so you should have everything you need."

Sharon followed Andrew and Gordie into the smallish room. The walls were lined with the crests and framed tartans of the Scottish families who'd settled in Glory in 1733— McGregor, Macdonough, Stewart and Campbell in the places of greatest honor.

Sharon circled the room to examine the majestic, nineteenth century painting that depicted Scottish sporting exhibitions, but

Andrew all but ignored them. He'd moved to the east wall and given his attention to five large unframed photographs—each three feet by two feet—of Glory Community Church's stained-glass windows.

"Five windows, five of Jesus' best-known parables," he said.

Sharon perched on the edge of the conference table and listened to Andrew orate. He seemed to enjoy speaking to an audience. Good. He would impress the elders tonight.

"First," Andrew went on, "is *The Prodigal Son,* everyone's favorite. The window depicts the delighted father celebrating the wayward son's return."

He gestured toward the second photograph. "The next depicts another familiar parable, *The Lost Sheep.*"

"That's also one of my favorites," Sharon joined in. "The shepherd has just found his one lost sheep, and in the distance we see the roughly ninety-nine he left alone while he went searching." She chuckled. "A supply pastor gave an especially dull sermon when Daniel Hartman was on his honeymoon. I actually counted the sheep in the window. There are only thirty-eight."

Andrew nodded. "But there are ten coins in the window that depicts the parable of *The Lost Coin.* A woman who lost one of ten precious silver coins rejoices when she finds it. The fourth window presents the parable of *The Wise and Foolish Builders.*"

"My turn," Sharon said. "A flood made of cobalt blue glass washes away the home of the foolish man who built his house on sand, but can't damage the house of the wise man who built atop a solid foundation."

"Finally, we have *The Pearl of Great Value,* the parable shown on the window that was destroyed by the fire," Andrew began again. "The illustration portrayed the merchant over-seeing the sale of his things so that he could purchase the prized pearl—which sits on a marble display stand near the top of the window. The pearl, of course, is the focal point of the illustration."

Andrew turned around to face Sharon and imitated the posture—complete with outstretched hands—of a preacher delivering a sermon. "*The Kingdom of Heaven* is like a merchant looking for fine pearls. When he found one of great value, he went away and sold everything he had and bought it. Matthew 13:45-46."

Sharon had expected Andrew to spout off about artistic merit, not grandly proclaim a Bible verse. She clapped appreciatively. "A man who quotes Scripture verbatim. I'm impressed."

He gave a theatrical bow. "Work with ecclesiastical glass long enough, and you can't help learning the best-known verses of the Bible."

Gordie chimed in. "What you said about the pearl being the focal point proved to be true in every way. Our fire chief said the pearl was the last part of the window to melt away."

Sharon recalled the day of the fire. She'd treated two firemen who had arrived at the E.R. with minor injuries. Both reported their astonishment that the fire crew had been able to contain the blaze to one narrow corner of the sanctuary. The fire had begun in a run of ancient electrical wiring directly below the window, and had traveled upward rather than sideways. *The Glory Gazette* reported this fact as "a stroke of great fortune," but many church members considered it a miracle.

Andrew gestured toward the wall. "These photographs are stunning," he said. "Who took them?"

"Lori Hartman," Gordie replied, "the Pastor's new wife. She took them last May, before they were married."

"You're lucky to have them. I can compare the colors on these photos with the surviving windows and figure out exactly the kind of glass used in the fifth window. They'll also help us with the painting."

Gordie stepped closer to the photos. "Now I get to ask my dumb question. I always thought that stained-glass windows were made of colored glass, not painted glass. Where did I go wrong?"

"You ended your journey of learning too early." Andrew pointed to the image of the pearl merchant. "Stained-glass windows are made of pieces of colored glass held together with lead strips called cames. But before we assemble the window, the fine details are painted on appropriate pieces of glass, which are then fired in a kiln to make the paint part of the glass surface." He tapped the merchant's face. "Ta-da! Painted stained glass."

Sharon slipped to her feet. "I'll get out of your way so you can think about your presentation."

Andrew waved a small black notebook. "You wouldn't let me have my laptop yesterday, but I never travel without this tucked into my jacket pocket. I did lots of thinking last night." He showed the inside of the notebook to Sharon. She could see one short sentence written in bold block letters.

"I have a simple recommendation to make to the elders," he said. "Duplicate the original window exactly."

"Is that possible?" Sharon asked.

"Absolutely! The original window was designed by a Scottish artist named Daniel Cottier and built by James Ballantine, my genuinely famous forebear. There's a stained-glass workshop in New Bern, North Carolina that can fabricate an identical window, if we provide the cartoon—the detailed blueprint and design drawing." Andrew smacked the notebook against his palm. "Now here's the really good news. The cartoon for the window is preserved in the Ballantine family archives."

"So that means we'll get our old window back…" Sharon said.

"…as if there'd never been a fire," Andrew replied.

"It seems a no-brainer," Gordie said excitedly. "Why would the church do anything else?"

"Why indeed?" Sharon felt like cheering. Andrew had come up with an easy-to-implement solution that would quickly erase all memories of the fire. The elders were bound to agree with such a straightforward recommendation and her life would become committee-less once again. With luck, before Christmas. That would be her "Pearl of Great Value."

Sharon pulled Gordie aside. "This is going to sound silly, but would you lock your front door today?"

"Way ahead of you. When Agent Keefe questioned me, he mentioned that Andrew might still be a target." He added with a frown, "I find that hard to believe in downtown Glory, *but*…"

Sharon nodded. "As the Scot's proverb says, 'better to keep the devil out, than have to put him out.'"

FOUR

Andrew stood in the back of Glory Community Church's sanctuary and counted heads. He tallied more than sixty people—a far larger audience than the "seven elders and a few members" Gordie had predicted.

"I'm astonished," Gordie said with a sheepish shrug. "Who knew that so many members cared enough about our window to attend a Tuesday evening meeting?"

"I like big audiences," Andrew said quickly to camouflage the twinge of concern he felt. If Gordie had been wrong about congregational interest in the window, what other incorrect information had the Windows Restoration Committee provided about the church and the project?

"Forget it! Committees never get everything right." He'd dealt with hundreds of church committees over the years. They were well-meaning, but because they were manned by inexperienced volunteers, they often ignored important minor details.

All the overhead lights were on, giving Andrew a better view than he'd had on Sunday of the recent fire's impact on the sanctuary. He noted dozens of plastered patches on the walls where new electrical wiring had been installed. A fitted panel made of several sheets of plywood neatly filled the opening that

had held the destroyed stained-glass window. And two rows of
classroom chairs substituted for a pair of pews that must have
been damaged. He guessed that the interior would be repainted
early in the New Year and after that the water-stained carpeting would be replaced.

Yet despite its under-construction ambiance, the sanctuary
still possessed great elegance—thanks largely to the four remaining stained-glass windows that overpowered the patched
walls and the other minor eyesores. Once again he experienced
a sense of pride at the legacy of excellence that James Ballantine had left to his descendents. It was a pity that James
hadn't traveled to America; he'd never had the chance to see
these magnificent fruits of his craftsmanship actually installed
in a church.

Sharon and Pastor Hartman were already sitting in the front
of the sanctuary, near the communion table. Andrew made his
way forward and sat down in the chair between them. Sharon's
black sweater brought out the gold in her complexion and her
hair. He found the contrast especially attractive. He reminded
himself to focus on his presentation—and the audience.

They were clustered in the first nine rows of pews and
seemed friendly enough, although he recognized only a handful
people he recalled from the tea party. He whispered to Sharon,
"I presume the elders are seated in the front pew."

"The elders, plus the other members of WinReC. In case
you've forgotten, Ann Trask Miller is the petite blonde sitting
with Gordie Pollack and Emma Neilson. She's the church's administrator—she reports to Pastor Hartman."

"Quite a crowd showed up."

"I told you that you're famous. There's even a reporter and
a photographer from the *Glory Gazette*." She added, "But don't

let it go to your head—or your heart. Your cardiac surveillance monitor will send bizarre signals to the hospital."

He glanced at his waist. His buttoned blazer hid the gizmo hanging on his belt. First thing tomorrow morning he'd return the monitor to the hospital and the oleander poisoning episode would be history. It had probably been some sort of ridiculous accident, anyway. Not even Special Agent Keefe had been able to invent a reason why anyone in Glory would want to kill him.

Andrew sensed motion to his right. He turned in time to see Daniel Hartman move behind the pulpit and adjust the microphone. The murmurings in the pews stopped.

"Good evening, my friends," Daniel said. "Let us as begin tonight's special meeting of our Elder Board with a prayer.

"Heavenly Father. In this period of Advent, Your servants at Glory Community Church await two things. First is the celebration of the birth of our Savior, second is the creation of a plan to complete the restoration of our sanctuary. The primary work left to be done is to replace the stained-glass window that was taken from us—a window that honors the teaching of Jesus of Nazareth.

"We thank You for the work done by the members of our Window Restoration Committee and for sending us an expert to guide their deliberations. We ask that You be with us this evening as we look ahead to a time when our place of worship will be renewed and restored. In Jesus' name we pray."

After a ringing "Amen!" from the audience, Daniel said, "Now I have the privilege of turning the microphone over to Sharon Pickard, the Chair of the WinReC, as everyone calls the Window Restoration Committee."

Andrew sat straight in his chair as Sharon replaced Daniel behind the podium. "Good evening, everyone," she said. "It is my great pleasure to introduce Dr. Andrew Ballantine—even though he rarely uses his title and prefers to be called Andrew."

She smiled warmly before continuing. "Andrew earned his Ph.D. in the History of Art from Cambridge University, in England. His area of research was British architecture—specifically the role of painted stained-glass windows in Scottish church architecture.

"It's not a cliché to say that Andrew wrote 'the book' on the subject." She held up a hefty volume. "And here's an interesting fact I didn't know before I read Andrew's book— Scotland has more original nineteenth-century stained-glass windows than any other European country. Many of those windows were built by James Ballantine, Andrew's great-great-great-grandfather—in the very same studio that crafted our windows."

Her eyes briefly met Andrew's as she scanned the audience. "Andrew frequently consults about painted stained glass. Over the years he has helped churches and cathedrals around the world maintain and repair their windows."

She paused for dramatic effect. "And now I am honored to present the esteemed Andrew Ballantine, who has graciously agreed to give us his recommendations for our window."

He stood up, received a smattering of applause—and made a snap decision. He didn't need the microphone; he would speak in front of the pulpit.

"It's a treat, ladies and gentlemen, for me to be here tonight." He gestured toward the four intact windows. "I vividly remember the first time I saw drawings of your windows. I was about ten years old—I browsed through an enormous scrapbook that was one of my grandfather's proudest possessions. The book had originally belonged to James Ballantine—it contained illustrations, most drawn by his own hand, of the many windows that the studios of Ballantine and Allen had built.

"Today, that scrapbook has become *my* proudest possession, and I think of the windows it depicts as my old friends. So you can imagine my delight when your WinReC invited me to be part of the team that will recommend how to properly restore the window on page 82 of my scrapbook."

Andrew paused to convey the full emotion he hoped to express. "Well, I have delightful news for the elders of Glory Community Church. As I told the Chair of WinReC today, you can fully restore *The Pearl of Great Value* window. Because we have the original design documents created by Daniel Cottier, the window can be recreated by a local stained-glass workshop. Your sanctuary will truly look good as new—as if the fire had never taken place." He tried for a genuinely warm expression. "I'd be delighted to answer any questions you have."

Someone standing behind the audience shot a flash photograph of him, and then took several other pictures of the sanctuary. Andrew stepped sideways as Pastor Hartman moved toward the pews, his outstretched hand holding a wireless microphone.

A stocky, red-headed elder stood up and took the mic. He cleared his throat and said, "Dr. Ballantine, my name is Gregory Grimes, but everyone calls me Greg. I shepherd Glory Community's Christian Education Team. My question is quite simple. Would it be possible to replace the damaged window with one that illustrates a different parable?"

"Pardon me?" Andrew said before he could stop himself.

Greg promptly restated his question. "You see, Dr. Ballantine, there are many of us who've never understood—and never liked—*The Pearl of Great Value* window. The church was sort of stuck with the old window, but the recent fire gave us a clean slate, so to speak. It seems to me that we now have a grand opportunity to find a parable we do like. How do we go about doing that?"

Andrew stared at Greg, struggling to respond. He finally said, "The damaged window was one of the loveliest ever built by the Ballantine Studios. We have the original artwork and can create an exact replica. Why would you want to replace the window with a different parable? How can one of Jesus' parables not work for you? Or the window that illustrates it?"

Another elder—a tall, thin man of about fifty—took the microphone from Greg. "I'll explain how. I've been a member of Glory Community for forty years, and that picture has always baffled me. When I was a kid, I thought *The Pearl of Great Value* was a baseball sitting on a pedestal. When I got older, and my teachers explained the parable, I couldn't understand why the man was selling all his stuff to buy a white blob. I've never seen anything spiritual in the illustration."

Andrew noted that Greg was nodding as the thin man spoke and that other elders were about to jump into the discussion. Surely one of them would describe Greg's notion as ridiculous.

A third elder—a man with thick white hair, who looked to be in his seventies—raised his hand. Andrew acknowledged him promptly. "Yes, sir. Do you have a question?"

"A comment, Dr. Ballantine. My name is Aaron DeWitt and I'm going to be both frank and honest. The parable itself is difficult for people to understand—at least it is for me. I don't know what to make of Jesus' words. Brandon, my nine-year-old grandson, talked to me about *The Pearl of Great Value* last night. He wants to enter the art contest and asked me what the parable means. I failed miserably trying to explain *why* the *Kingdom of Heaven* is like a man searching for a pearl of great value.

"I'm not happy that our window was destroyed, but I consider the damage providential. To build on what Greg said, we now have an opportunity to choose a parable that illustrates one of Jesus' teachings that the whole church will find meaningful."

Several people began to clap. A moment later most of the audience was enthusiastically applauding the elderly elder.

Andrew peered over his shoulder at Gordie. His eyes were open wide, his expression startled, as if he'd been watching a horror movie. Andrew didn't dare to look at Sharon, who must've been even more appalled by what had just happened.

Get back on your horse! Change their minds.

He smiled at Aaron DeWitt. "Stained-glass windows are often symbolic—they require that the viewer think about their meaning. That's part of the delight of stained-glass as an art form. Please remember that your windows are true works of art, not merely illustrations of Bible stories."

"Begging your pardon, Dr. Ballantine, but I've been thinking about *The Pearl of Great Value* window for longer than you've been alive. That's enough time for even a non-artist like me to figure out that the illustration is muddled rather than symbolic."

Andrew managed to maintain a neutral face as the white-haired man earned a fresh round of applause.

Andrew waited for quiet to return and then said, "When Sharon introduced me, she told you that I have a good deal of…*experience* with historic painted-glass windows. Well, one thing my experience tells me for sure is that when Daniel Cottier created the windows back during the middle of the nineteenth century, he designed the five of them to work together. The window destroyed by the fire was part of a larger artistic treasure. You are its stewards—the people responsible for maintaining the artistic integrity of Glory Community Church."

"Maybe so," Greg said, "but I see things, the primary purpose of our windows is to educate the people who sit in this sanctuary. I'm less concerned with keeping art historians happy than I am with enhancing the lives of the members of Glory Community Church."

Andrew heard Gordie groan behind him. He ignored the plaintive sound and pressed on. "I'm confident that Daniel Cottier had much the same thought in mind when he drew the cartoons for the five windows. He understood the power of art to convey Christian truth. It's not by accident that Cottier is regarded as one of the great stained-glass artists of all time.

"I strongly recommend against a counterfeit design—especially when we have the ability to reproduce Cottier's original window. Doing anything less would be equivalent to throwing away a masterpiece."

"I agree!" a woman said. Andrew spotted her sitting in the third pew. She wasn't an elder, but she seemed to be on his side. He pointed at her.

"I'm not a member of Glory Community Church," she said. "I represent the Glory Historical Commission—the municipal agency responsible for protecting Glory's architectural landmarks. I can't speak for the other commissioners, but I'd be opposed to giving this church our okay to abandon an important part of Glory's cultural heritage.

"And let's not forget that many visitors include Glory Community Church's stained-glass windows on their itinerary of sights to see. It would be a shame to diminish one of Glory's leading tourist attractions by replacing an acknowledged work of art with an imitation."

Several people in the audience booed. A fourth elder leapt

to his feet. "The elders of Glory Community will do what we think is best for the church."

A new round of applause was accompanied by several flashes as the photographer took more pictures, but this time Pastor Hartman silenced the audience. "Everyone—please remember that this is a special meeting of our elders, not a political rally. I believe that we were discussing Daniel Cottier."

A fifth elder rose, a bearded man whom Andrew had met at the tea party. Andrew recalled the man had introduced himself as the owner of an art gallery in Glory. Certainly, he would understand the importance of honoring Daniel Cottier's artistic conception.

"Cottier is justly famous for the fine work he did," the man said, "but merely because an artist is well-known doesn't mean that he hit a home run every time he went to bat. I think Cottier blew it when he designed our fifth window. You consider *The Pearl of Great Value* a masterpiece, Dr. Ballantine, but to most of us it's a rather mediocre window—a confusing illustration that we can easily do without."

Before Andrew could respond, Greg took charge. "Some of us had hoped to make a decision tonight, but it's clear to me that the Elder Board has a lot more thinking to do. Therefore, I move that we postpone the vote on restoring the window so that each of us can fully consider what we've heard from Dr. Ballantine and the other speakers—along with any other advice WinReC has for us."

Someone seconded the motion. Andrew scarcely paid attention as Daniel Hartman orchestrated a quick vote. The motion to postpone passed unanimously.

Andrew felt a hand grasp his arm. He turned and looked into Sharon's stunned eyes. "I'm sorry, Andrew," she said. "I had no idea so many elders…" She hesitated.

He finished her sentence. "…hated my great-great-great-grandfather's window."

She shrugged. There seemed nothing more for either of them to say.

He smiled at her. "I'm going to walk back to The Scottish Captain. Don't even try to change my mind. I need some time alone—and I don't care about my cardiac surveillance system. If my heart was going to go berserk, it would have happened five minutes ago."

She shrugged again.

He walked toward the narthex, doing his best to forget the grim look on Sharon Pickard's face.

She apologized to me, but we both know that I let her down.

FIVE

Sharon bicycled south on Broad Street toward The Scottish Captain, her head down, her collar up. A stinging wind blew off Albemarle Sound, causing the "Christmas—a Season of Glory" banners suspended between the power poles to twist and sway above her head.

And then it began to rain.

Sharon pedaled faster, wishing that she'd driven to tonight's meeting. She soon found herself laughing out loud. Frigid rain drops trickling down her neck provided the perfect finale to an especially difficult Wednesday.

The day had begun with a call from Agent Keefe, who informed her that the forensic tests were complete and there was absolutely no doubt that her dessert had poisoned Andrew Ballantine. Moreover, her fingerprints had been found on the dish that contained the oleander toxin. His parting words were, "Would you like to change your account of what happened at the tea party?"

Unfortunately, when she threw her cell phone against the wall, the circuitry hiccoughed, resetting the memory and erasing all the numbers stored in the internal address book. And then after breakfast, she had to listen to three sets of moans and groans from the other members of the Window Restoration Committee when she organized a last-minute meeting to recover from last night's unexpected brouhaha at Glory Community Church. To top the misery off, she'd spent her free time that day trying to decide who was right—Andrew or the elders—and had confused herself even more in the process.

The Pearl of Great Value had become a *Pain of Great Intensity*—mostly because both sides of the argument were logical and reasonable.

On one hand, Andrew Ballantine had raised sensible issues of artistic merit, cultural legacy and historical stewardship.

On the other hand, the cantankerous elders who disliked the old window had provided equally compelling evidence that the illustration—and the parable—didn't "work" for them.

And so, what should have been a quick get-together in the sanctuary to rubber-stamp a straightforward suggestion had turned into a battle of competing values—both equally worthwhile.

Where's King Solomon when we need him?

Sharon hefted her bike up the Captain's three front steps and leaned it against the porch railing. She brushed the raindrops off her hair, took a moment to examine the stunning imported Christmas wreath Emma had hung on the front door, then rang the bell. The door swung open; Emma Neilson handed her a towel.

"I guessed you'd be pigheaded enough to bicycle all the way from Queen Street on a bleak evening," Emma said.

"Not pigheaded—merely crabby. I wanted to exercise off some of the annoyance of a really rotten day."

"Give me your jacket—you're dripping on my rug." Emma added, "Your day's not over yet."

"I can't stand much more excitement. What's going on?"

"You may find this hard to believe, but Gordie and Ann have taken different sides."

"Oh, no!"

"Oh, yes. He's become a clone of Andrew Ballantine, while Ann now supports the elders who spoke last night." Emma chuckled. "It started the moment they arrived. They're expressing their exasperation with each other by wolfing down the oatmeal raisin cookies Calvin made for us. I shamed them into leaving one or two small ones for you."

She put her hand on Sharon's shoulder. "Before we go in… I'm dying of curiosity. Rafe doesn't tell me anything about the investigation. How's Agent Keefe doing?"

"Not very well, if I read his tone of voice right. I seem to be his best, and only, suspect."

Emma grimaced. "I know that Ty is smarter than that."

"Maybe. But if he doesn't make any progress soon, I'll turn myself into a detective."

Emma laughed. "Now that I'm married to Rafe, I have to try to dissuade you. What can you accomplish that he can't?"

"Beats me…but I was at the tea party, he wasn't."

She walked with Emma into the small rear parlor, the room at the Captain that Sharon loved most. Emma had filled the parlor with antique Victorian furnishings that created a time capsule from England in the 1880s: Overstuffed sofas and wing chairs, mahogany buffet and pivot-top game table, a red, beige and green Oriental rug, and an unusual collection of mid-nineteenth century oil lamps.

Tonight, the vintage furnishings seemed embraced by an unpleasant heaviness. The frustration oozing from Ann and Gordie was strong enough for Sharon to feel. Ann sat alone on a purple damask-covered settee, peering unkindly at Gordie; he had staked out a leather-upholstered side chair and was glaring back at Ann over the steaming mug he held in both hands.

"Hi, gang," Sharon said cheerfully. "Thanks for giving up another evening."

Both Ann and Gordie replied with indifferent shrugs. Emma rolled her eyes then made a "what do we do now?" face.

"Okay guys," Sharon said. "Snap out of it. We have to help the elders find a way around the disagreement. The last thing we need is a fight of our own to slow us down."

"There's only one *proper* thing for the elders to do," Gordie said. "They must follow the sage advice offered by Andrew Ballantine and rebuild the window that inspired Glory Community Church for more than one hundred fifty years."

"If that's the 'proper thing,'" Ann said, "the church might as well save its money and leave the plywood panels in place. They're as effective at communicating Jesus' teaching as the original window was."

"Phooey!" Gordie said.

"Double phooey!" Ann replied.

"Heavenly Father," Sharon said, "we thank You for the considerable progress this committee has made. We ask for the wisdom and patience to complete our assignment." She paused. "And we have one more request… Although we come together as Your children this evening, please help us to act like adults. In Jesus name we pray. Amen."

Emma echoed a loud "Amen," Ann snickered, and Gordie managed to stifle a chortle.

Progress! Sharon thought. The more they laugh, the less they'll bicker. She dropped into a wing chair and said, "We seem to be the middle of a muddle."

"I'll say!" Gordie replied. "Poor Andrew Ballantine was sandbagged by a surprise attack last night. That wouldn't have happened if the WinReC member best situated to appreciate the elders' foibles had seen fit to warn us in advance of their…ah, *concerns.*"

Ann poked her tongue out at Gordie. "Working at the church doesn't make me an expert on what the elders are thinking. You're our historian—why didn't you know that so many church members have been unhappy with the window for decades?"

"I'm glad you asked! In all my years as a member of Glory Community Church, I didn't hear a single grumble about *The Pearl of Great Value*—the parable or the window."

"Mommy! Ann and Gordie are fighting again," Emma said in a singsongy voice.

"Put a sock in it—both of you!" Sharon said. "Forget about last night. We have to look to the future and come up with a compromise that both camps can live with—a middle ground position that keeps everyone happy. Including Andrew Ballantine."

"Simple to talk about, hard to achieve," Emma said. "I don't see a merry middle ground in this mess. The elders seem to have two choices—restore the original window or switch to a different parable and design a new window. Either way, some folks will be unhappy when they come to church."

Emma passed the cookie plate to Sharon. There was one oversize cookie left. She broke it in two and took the slightly smaller piece. Half of one Calvin Constable creation was as rich as three store-bought cookies.

"And on the subject of Andrew…" Emma handed Sharon a mugful of hot spiced cider. "He's upstairs in his room. Shouldn't our consultant be a part of this conversation?"

Sharon gazed at the mug so that she didn't have to look into

Emma's eyes. The thought of Andrew less than a hundred feet away made her want to race up the stairs, even though her pride wouldn't let her. Not after what he'd said to her today. "We'll involve Andrew later," she said. "I'd rather the WinReC think about a compromise on our own first."

Emma's skeptical expression shouted her disbelief, even though she was too polite to press Sharon for giving an improbable answer to a simple question. *Thank goodness for that.* No way could she explain her real reason for not inviting Andrew.

He'd shown up unexpectedly at the hospital that morning and invited her to breakfast in the cafeteria. He'd seemed surprisingly upbeat considering the events of the night before. They chattered about Glory, and Christmas shopping yet to be done, and the likelihood of a white Christmas in coastal North Carolina and even about the enemies he hadn't realized he'd made—people who might have come to Glory and poisoned him. But then she'd made the mistake of talking about compromise.

"Compromise with what?" he'd said brusquely, an indignant frown spilling across his face. "Are you suggesting that the church negotiates away the artistic integrity of a renowned window created by a great artist?"

"That's not what I mean by finding a middle ground."

To her surprise, his scowl faded and he gently touched the top of her hand. "Sharon, forgive me for snapping at you. I'm still mad at myself for what happened at the meeting. I wasn't prepared to defend *The Pearl of Great Value,* but I will be the next time I meet with the elders. I'll spend today, and tomorrow if necessary, building my case. I owe that much to the lovely window."

"Actually—I've been thinking about the scrapbook you described to the elders."

"I wish I'd brought it with me to Glory. It would help you understand why I feel the way I do about the windows James Ballantine built."

"How many of the windows in the book were designed by Daniel Cottier?"

"More than fifty. Why do you ask?"

"Well, with fifty-plus windows in the book, it's probable that Daniel Cottier designed stained-glass window cartoons for more than five different parables. After all, Jesus spoke thirty-three parables and roughly the same number of parable-like proverbs." She'd smiled at him. "I looked that up—on the Internet."

Andrew didn't return her smile. "So why not let the elders browse through the scrapbook and choose another Cottier window that they like better than *The Pearl of Great Value?*"

She tried not to look sheepish. "That seems a workable solution to me—a Cottier window with a parable that our elders will support."

He shook his head in annoyance. "There are a thousand reasons why dropping in a different Daniel Cottier design is a terrible idea. To begin with, it won't match the four other windows. A new design will likely introduce changes in the shapes of the glass segments, the colors and the surface textures. Cottier designed Glory Community's five windows as a set."

"I see."

"No. I'm afraid that you don't see. The name of your team is the Window *Restoration* Committee. 'Restoration' means re-turning something to its original condition. That's what you set out to do—and that's what I agreed to help you do."

She'd watched Andrew leave, wishing that she'd argued more forcefully for some sort of compromise. She may have proposed a "terrible" idea, but he'd been too stubborn to invent an alternative that would work. "You gave in quickly," she murmured to herself, "because you didn't want him to abandon Glory and rush back to Asheville. And because those confused emotions of yours have become even more puzzling."

Her initial attraction to Andrew was certainly based on his physical appearance. He was a startlingly handsome man. That gave way quickly to a more sensible appeal based on his charm and intellect. But now something new had arrived on the scene. The way Andrew believed in the old window shouted that he was a man of considerable integrity. And integrity was only a hop, skip and jump away from trustworthiness.

It may be that Andrew has the fidelity you thought you'd never find again.

"Earth calling Sharon," Emma said.

Sharon realized that Emma was staring at her. "Sorry about that. I was thinking about the challenge of finding the middle ground."

"The middle is often wishy-washy and wimpy," Gordie said, "a refuge for people who can't make up their minds."

"This time I agree with our Scotsman," Ann said. "Are you for the original window…or against it?"

Sharon crossed her arms over her chest. "To be honest, that's a decision I don't intend to make. I don't have to take sides, so I won't."

"Spoken like a true committee chairperson," Gordie said.

"The thing that troubles me most about the fight is that I haven't thought the dilemma through," Sharon went on. "I suppose I know what Andrew means when he talks about artistic integrity. The ruined window represents a lost master-piece that we can bring back to life. So why would we do anything else? After all, if the wiring hadn't caught fire, no one would suggest that we destroy *The Pearl of Great Value.*"

"Well said!" Gordie exclaimed.

"But there was a fire," Ann chimed in, "and that makes all the difference."

Sharon nodded. "Because the fire destroyed the window, we now have the ability to do something new."

"Much *more* than the ability," Ann said. "Along with the opportunity, we have the responsibility to build a better window this time around. A window that our congregants will truly love."

"I'll bet the congregants alive in 1858 loved the original window," Gordie said. "We have to assume that *The Pearl of Great Value* was a favorite parable within the church back then. Or else, why would the elders commission a stained-glass window to illustrate it?"

"That's a fascinating point," Sharon said. "Did church members in the nineteenth century understand the parable better than we do today?"

"Probably," Ann said, "but only because most of the members back then belonged to one church their whole lives."

"You've lost me," Gordie said.

Ann took the remaining half of the last cookie. "Jesus never explained the meaning of *The Pearl of Great Value.* Consequently, different people, different pastors, all cook up different interpretations. Our members come from many Christian traditions, so we have lots of 'meanings' floating around Glory Community. That's what causes the confusion we heard expressed last night."

Gordie shook his head. "I still don't get it."

"Okay. What's your explanation of the parable?"

"*Obviously,*" he said, "*The Pearl of Great Value* is Jesus. The merchant represents humanity. Each of us should be willing to give up everything we have to gain Jesus."

"Whoa!" Ann shouted, "There's nothing obvious about your interpretation. I was taught that Jesus is the merchant. He gave up everything He had to ransom humanity, the Pearl, from sin."

"Oh, boy," Emma said. "You're making my head spin."

"Isn't there a preferred explanation?"

"Absolutely!" Ann said with a laugh. "Every member of Glory Community prefers his or her interpretation. That was Pastor Hartman's answer when I asked him the same question this morning."

"Nonetheless," Sharon said, "we need to find compromise— an approach that will give us artistic integrity *and* happy elders."

"And also prevent conflict," Emma said. "Don't forget that. Glory Community has been through lots of pain recently—the last thing the church needs is a new disagreement over a stained-glass window."

"On that scary note," Sharon said, "I'm out of here."

She accompanied Emma to the front door and retrieved her red all-weather jacket from the coatrack.

"It's still raining," Emma said.

"I like biking in the rain. It's refreshing."

Emma made a face. "A half mile of cold, wet refreshment."

"I'll be fine." Sharon zipped her jacket and tugged the hood over her head.

"You'll be fine, but I'll feel guilty that Andrew doesn't know you're here. He likes you—I can see it in his eyes when he talks about you. He'll be upset that you didn't give him a chance to say hello."

"I have to get home."

"Do you realize you're blushing?"

"I am not."

"Oh, yes you are."

Sharon knew that Emma was right. She could feel the heat on her cheeks. She pulled open the front door, strode onto the porch and nearly walked into Andrew Ballantine.

He was aiming a flashlight beam at the back of an SUV parked on the street, illuminating a multipurpose utility pack attached to the spare tire holder. She saw her bike hanging on the aluminum hooks, secured in place with a bungee cord.

"I'll drive you and your bicycle home," he said.

There seemed no graceful way of refusing his offer. She mumbled, "Isn't my town house out of your way?"

"Completely out of the way." He grinned. "My room is upstairs."

She cringed at the inanity of what she'd said, although Andrew seemed not to mind her sudden attack of tongue-tiedness. He pressed a button on his key fob. The SUV's lights flashed on with a beep.

She let him lead her into the rain.

SIX

Andrew found a parking spot near the Captain's back door and switched off the engine. He listened to the rain drumming on the SUV's roof and thought about his brief journey to the other side of Glory.

Sharon had given him curt directions to her home on Queen Street. Neither of them had spoken during the quick trip. When they arrived, she'd pointed at a row of town houses squeezed into the short block between Albemarle Street and Oliver Street. "I own the one in the middle. You can park in front."

She'd quickly slipped out of the passenger seat and retrieved her bicycle from the rack. She'd thanked him and said goodnight. All with more politeness than warmth.

Well, how did he expect her to act?

Sharon was upset with him—with good reason. Breakfast at the hospital with her had not been his finest hour. He'd spent most of the day fretting about the angry things he'd said to her, and feeling guilty for storming off like a petulant adolescent.

It was one more example of his "obsession" with his work getting in the way of a promising relationship. It had happened again and again over the years, despite his efforts to control it. His love for church architecture, his admiration for stained-glass windows, made him fight with the women who challenged his decisions.

He had no excuses for his bad behavior, but he did have an explanation to offer Sharon, a reason that might help her understand the way his mind worked—assuming she still cared. Her unexpected mention of compromise had stunned him. The first thought that had popped into his mind was, how could an intelligent woman talk about a "middle ground" when the proper course of action was as clear as a piece of untextured stained glass?

The Pearl of Great Value window was a masterpiece, regardless of its educational value. And it was ridiculous to throw a masterpiece away on such flimsy grounds. Imagine the owners refusing to restore Leonardo da Vinci's *Last Supper* because some onlookers were confused by the fast-paced events described in Luke 22:7–20.

Instead of keeping his own counsel, he'd shot his mouth off this morning. But he'd wisely kept his thoughts to himself during the short drive across Glory through lashing rain. With equal wisdom, he hadn't asked Sharon why she chose not to invite him to tonight's meeting of the Windows Restoration Committee.

He'd been sitting in the front parlor when Gordie Pollack and Ann Trask Miller had arrived shortly before seven o'clock. It didn't take a rocket scientist to figure out that the members of WinReC were gathering at The Scottish Captain to talk about the window—without him.

Surprisingly, he'd felt more relieved than snubbed at the time. The enthusiasm Andrew had brought to Glory was slowly being swamped by the gnawing suspicion that the elders would do the wrong thing in the end. They seemed determined to find a new illustration, no matter how zealously he championed James Ballantine's beautiful window.

And yet, it wasn't his nature to walk away from a fight when he was so plainly in the right. He'd keep pressing to save *The Pearl of Great Value,* even if he couldn't win.

A low-slung car parked next to his SUV and a moment later someone tapped on his fogged-up side window. The power windows didn't work with the engine turned off, so he opened the driver side door. Rafe Neilson stood holding an oversize umbrella. Behind him was his vintage Corvette.

"Can you spare a minute?" Rafe said. "I'd like to talk to you."

Andrew slid out of the driver's seat and followed Rafe along a stone path into The Scottish Captain's kitchen.

"Coffee?" Rafe asked.

Andrew nodded. "I'd love a cup."

Rafe moved to the coffeemaker on the back counter and filled two mugs.

"I just spent an hour listening to Special Agent Ty Keefe whine and whimper about his investigation. He's been stuck on square one since Monday morning, with a clear case of attempted murder, but no prime suspect. Anyone at the tea party could've poured oleander toxin on your dessert. He claims that you haven't been as cooperative as he'd hoped."

"What a joke! I've told him everything I know—which is nothing."

"I've known Ty Keefe for years. He can be annoying. But keep in mind where he's coming from on this case. He knows that he can't make any progress until he figures out why someone would want to poison a visiting stained-glass guru." Rafe smiled. "I feel his pain. It's hard to solve a murder without a hint of a motive."

Rafe flipped a light switch. Several floodlights came on in the back garden, illuminating the gazebo and making it visible through the windows behind the sink. The falling rain transformed the white wooden octagon into a ghostly structure that seemed to hang in the air above the dark ground.

"The scene of the crime," Andrew said.

"Perhaps—although we're not even sure of that. All we can say for sure is that an unknown person poisoned your… What's the name of the pear pudding that Sharon Pickard made?"

"Strathbogie Mist."

"Sounds like the name of a ski run on a friendly mountain. Well, your helping of Mist might have been poisoned in the gazebo or possibly back here in the kitchen."

Andrew shrugged. "I didn't see a thing."

"Nor did any of the other dozen witnesses who Ty interviewed. They all tell the same story. No one saw anybody tamper with any of the ramekins. No one knew you before that afternoon. No one has any link to Asheville or to stained-glass windows. No one had a reason to want you dead." Rafe's deepset hazel eyes seemed intent as they studied Andrew. "Are you certain that you have no enemies in North Carolina?"

"I didn't have any on Sunday. But after what happened at the church last night, I wouldn't be surprised if the combined Elder Board and WinReC were gunning for me."

Rafe laughed. "Emma told me about the special meeting. However, we're more concerned about the person who tried to kill you two days earlier, on Sunday afternoon. He or she chose a rather unusual method that required advance preparation. The residue in the ceramic ramekin Ty had tested contained an unusually high concentration of toxin. Whoever prepared the oleander extract was an expert—and took the time to do it right. You survived because you received prompt medical care and because you're in such good shape."

Andrew hoped that Rafe didn't see him shudder. He'd tried to put his near-death out of his mind, refusing to believe that anyone had made a sincere attempt to murder him. But how else could he explain a lethal dose of carefully prepared oleander poison finding its way into his helping of Strathbogie Mist?

"I don't have any enemies anywhere—at least, none that I know of."

"I hope you're right, because Ty is about to shift his investigation into low gear. He's out of suspects and ideas, and has other cases to work." He swallowed the last gulp of his coffee. "Whoever poisoned you is still out there and…"

"Free to cook up more oleander toxin," Andrew finished.

"Precisely." Rafe put his empty mug in the sink. "Have you eaten dinner yet?"

"Nope. I've heard that The Glorious Catch on Dock Street serves the best seafood in town."

"It does, but I have a better idea. Dine with Emma and me tonight."

"You're sure Emma won't mind?"

"In truth, you'll be helping her. Tonight is sample night. We're going to try two of Calvin Constable's experimental creations. Emma loves to have an unbiased guinea pig at the table, because I start out skeptical of anything Calvin concocts without a proven recipe." He leaned forward and lowered his voice. "He's an incredible cook, but a warped inventor—a mad kitchen scientist."

Andrew lifted his mug in a pretend toast to Rafe. "When you put it that way…how can I refuse? Although let's not forget what happened the last time I ate 'experimental food' at the Captain."

"Ouch!" Rafe said with another laugh. "Calvin has made some weird dishes, but he's never cooked with oleander."

A metallic squeak behind Andrew caught his ear. He turned as Amanda Turner pushed open the swinging door that connected with the Captain's first-floor hallway. Her eyes widened when she saw him.

"Oops! I thought the kitchen was empty. I smelled coffee from a distance—I need a cup desperately."

"That's an easy problem to fix," Rafe said. He filled a mug and handed it to her. "Amanda, you've met Andrew Ballantine, haven't you?"

"Absolutely. We're old friends." She emphasized her peculiar notion of friendship by winking at Andrew.

She sat on the edge of the kitchen table, seemingly in a mood to join their conversation.

"How goes the redecoration of The Robert Burns Inn?" Rafe asked. Andrew noted a sudden sharpness in his voice.

Amanda sighed heavily. "The contractors have promised me that the walls will be painted and the new carpeting down before Christmas Day. I hope they've told me the truth, because I've started to accept reservations for New Year's Eve getaways." She peered intently at Rafe. "I don't have to tell you that every day without paying guests costs a B and B dearly. Our fixed costs each month are significant."

"I suppose so." Andrew noted that Rafe was looking at the floor, not at Amanda. Perhaps he didn't like the woman, either?

She abruptly turned toward Andrew. "You've been working with Glory Community Church—what's the place like?"

"Um…in what regard?"

"I'm looking for a church where I can attend Christmas Eve services. Emma told me that Pastor Hartman is worth hearing, but I'm tired of looking at in-progress construction work. I see ladders and scaffolding whenever I visit the Bobby Burns—I don't need to see more in church on Christmas Eve. Is Glory Community finished?" She smiled. "Emma assures me I'll enjoy the service and the sanctuary, but I'd appreciate a second opinion."

Andrew glanced at Rafe for guidance, but he was still staring at the floor. "Well," he finally said, "if I'm still in Glory on Christmas Eve, I plan to attend the service at Glory Community Church."

"In that case, maybe I'll join you. We can go together."

"Hmm. That's a thought," Andrew murmured.

"I'll hold you to it."

"I'm sure you'll try," he mumbled under his breath.

"I'll be off," she said, "and leave you two hunky men alone."

"Have a good night," Andrew said as she left. He waited for the sound of her footfalls to recede in the distance, and then uttered a windy, "Whew!"

"You clearly have a new admirer," Rafe said. "I didn't know that you two had a thing going."

"Bite your tongue. She's supposed to be married, but she keeps flirting with me. I'm half-afraid to pass her on the staircase when I go to my room." He pointed toward the second floor to emphasize his predicament. "It began on Sunday afternoon."

"How could you tell? You were mostly unconscious on Sunday."

"She ambushed me outside the gazebo before the tea party began." He tried to imitate her drawl. "You may think I'm taken, sugar. But the fact is that Mr. Harrison Turner of Birmingham, Alabama, is a hard-workin' travelin' man who has made a fine livin' sellin' laboratory equipment to hospitals and doctor's offices. The man's simply not interested in B and Bs. He'll be a thousand miles away from Glory for the foreseeable future."

Rafe laughed louder than before. "When a woman like Amanda sees a man she wants, she puts the pedal to the metal and goes after him." He went on. "I should be a tad put off. She hasn't flirted with me."

"She wouldn't dare. Emma would flatten her."

"You bet I would." Emma pushed past the door and gave Rafe a welcoming kiss. "I presume you were talking about Amanda Turner."

He nodded. "Our resident spy is also a flirt."

She glared at Rafe and spoke to Andrew. "Don't listen to Rafe. He loves to exaggerate."

"No, I'm not," Rafe said. "She put the moves on poor Andrew—after she tried to pump me for more information about The Scottish Captain."

Emma shook her head sadly. "Rafe doesn't like Amanda," she said to Andrew. "But she asks the kinds of questions that every new B and B owner needs answers to."

"Sure!" Rafe said. "Such as the nitty-gritty financial details behind the Captain's operations, which will help her compete with us more effectively. I've seen her browse through our linen cupboards, check out our furnace and inventory the food in our pantry. She's a snoop."

"Amanda's nervous—she made a major investment and now she's spending lots more money to redecorate the place. I had the same worries after I bought this place."

"Yeah. But you paid top dollar for the Captain. Everyone in Glory knows that Amanda got the Bobby Burns at a fire-sale price after Bill Dorsey died," Rafe said.

"True. But Carol Dorsey couldn't run the place by herself,

so she accepted the first offer that came along. Besides, the inn was full of terrible memories. She wanted out."

Andrew must have looked bewildered, because Emma explained, "Bill Dorsey had a heart attack and died in his sleep. He was stone cold when Carol woke up next to him in the morning."

"By the way…" Rafe said. "I've invited Andrew to dinner. You can lock the kitchen door."

"Did you warn him what to expect tonight?" She pushed home a bolt that pinned the swinging door shut.

"I provided complete disclosure." He chuckled. "But in spite of my brutal honesty, he's still willing to sample Calvin's untested cuisine."

Rafe said a blessing as Emma served up the first experiment. "Highland Quiche is a variation of traditional Quiche Lorraine that is made without a crust. Calvin created an original recipe based on eggs, cream, Ayrshire bacon, Scottish smoked salmon and Tobermory Cheddar cheese. This is the Sunday brunch version—served with a salad and plenty of crusty French bread."

"I stopped at three helpings," Andrew said when they'd finished eating, "only because there wasn't a fourth on the plate."

"I concur," Rafe said. "Scottish Quiche is magnificent. I may be forced to take back every critical comment I've made about Calvin's creations. I might even forget the time he tried to merge Scottish and Chinese food for Gordie Pollack's birthday party, and came up with Haggis Szechuan-style and Shrimp-Fried Oats." He added, "What's for dessert?"

"Dundee *Buche de Noel,*" Emma replied. "It's an elaborate French cake shaped to look like a traditional Yule Log. There's rolled yellow sponge cake inside and thick chocolate buttercream frosting on the outside."

Rafe took a large slice. "Testing dessert is a thankless job, but someone has to do it."

"What do you think?" Emma said when Andrew had polished off his slice.

Rafe answered first. "I have to tell the truth. This is not my favorite Calvin dessert. It tastes like Christmas fruitcake."

"Yes, it does!" Andrew exclaimed. "And that's why I think it's extraordinary—one of the best cakes I've ever eaten." He waved his fork at Rafe. "Pay attention. This is Dundee *Buche de Noel.* Dundee cake is Scottish fruitcake, a treat usually covered with almonds. Your genius chef has melded the best aspects of the French and Scottish confections—even adding almonds to the chocolate buttercream."

"I remain unimpressed," Rafe said. "Fruitcake is…*fruitcake.*"

"Then you don't get another slice." Emma put a second piece on Andrew's plate. "Enough talk about food. What do you think about Sharon Pickard?"

Rafe groaned loudly. "My wife loves to play matchmaker. Single people run from her on the streets of Glory. I advise you to flee as fast as you can."

Emma waved her fingers dismissively at Rafe and pressed on. "Sharon is a delightful woman. Sincere, brilliant, personable and beautiful."

"Not to mention your best friend in Glory," Rafe quipped.

"Exactly," Emma said with a crisp nod. "She's my friend because she's exceptional in every respect." She used her index finger to prod Andrew's arm. "Sorry. I neglected to mention her musical talent. Sharon is a superb singer—probably the best alto in the choir."

"She didn't tell me about her singing."

"Of course not. Sharon will be upset if she learns you found out from me, but she took a leave of absence from the choir and didn't perform in Glory's production of *The Messiah* because she knew that the WinReC meetings would interfere with rehearsals." Emma gave his arm another prod. "She's dependable and conscientious."

Andrew smiled at Emma. "Well, I agree that Sharon is special, but I'm not sure she feels that way about me."

Emma scowled. "Puh-lease! Think about Sunday afternoon in the gazebo. The pair of you generated enough electricity to light Glory."

Rafe groaned again, but Andrew noted that he didn't challenge what Emma had said.

All Andrew could do was shrug. The Neilsons didn't know about the powerful wedge prying Sharon away from him. He would never agree to compromise. She believed in the middle ground—a way of restoring Glory Community's stained-glass window that would keep everyone happy. He rejected the idea out of hand.

Another fight over *The Pearl of Great Value* would short-circuit any electricity that remained in their relationship. But a fresh argument was inevitable, because he would be the one to start it. Sooner or later, Sharon would ask the inevitable question: What comes first—me, or your career? He would hem and haw, but she would figure out what every other woman he'd gotten close to had learned: His work was ultimately what he valued most in his life.

It was too late for him to change. Why even try?

SEVEN

He can't say I didn't warn him. I told him I'm an impatient person and not diplomatic.

Sharon chained her bicycle to the rack in front of Snacks of Glory and checked her reflection in the restaurant's front window as she brushed her windblown hair and moistened her lips with lip gloss.

She'd sounded like a harridan when Pastor Hartman had called a few moments after she'd stepped out of the shower— she didn't have to look like one, too.

Poor Daniel. I let him have it with both barrels.

Of course she'd apologized almost immediately for chewing his head off. Of course she'd agreed to meet him for breakfast to discuss an "issue that arose last night over the stained-glass window."

What must he think of me for making a fuss over such a simple request?

She moved to the glass entrance door, pushed the silver Christmas wreath aside, peered into the restaurant and spotted Daniel's reddish-brown hair at once. He was sitting alone at a table for two in the back corner. Daniel was almost fifty but looked a decade younger. He seemed in a good mood from a distance, not angry at anyone. But then, pastors were expected to maintain their cool, even when overburdened members of their flocks acted like jerks on the telephone.

She pulled the door open and stepped inside. He waved when he saw her. He smiled when she reached him and, to her astonishment, said, "I hope you'll forgive me for bugging you at the crack of dawn."

"It's the other way around. You need to forgive me for barking at you this morning."

"I deserved to be barked at." His smile faded into a guilt-filled grimace. "You reminded me of two things I never should have forgotten—that you've given a month of free time to our window and that you have other things in your life besides the Window Restoration Committee."

Sharon sat down and realized that up close Daniel looked tense, under strain. He'd been an Army Chaplain who'd served in combat and later rose to the rank of colonel. Not much at Glory Community Church fazed him. The "issue" on his mind today must be a doozie.

"What happened last night?" she asked.

"I'll tell you after we order. Snacks of Glory invented a new line of breakfast sandwiches. My favorite is the SOGgy Benedict."

She laughed. "How can I resist a name like that?"

"Don't even try. Surrender is inevitable." He signaled the waitress, a plump redhead shoehorned into a slightly tight Christmas elf outfit, but still wearing an encouraging smile.

"The usual?" she asked.

"Big Benedict Breakfasts for two." After the waitress left, he said, "Have you browsed through the statues across the street in Founders' Park?"

"I've seen Moira McGregor and her husband, Duncan. Why do you ask?"

"Well, I found myself wondering this morning what Moira, Duncan and the rest of the clan would say about our stained-glass window. Glory's first residents in the eighteenth century had to deal with epidemics and famines, and droughts, not to mention crop failures, and revolution and highway robbery. What would they think about us starting a major controversy over something that isn't all that important?"

"Now I'm really curious. What's going on?"

Daniel sighed heavily. "I received this e-mail message last night." He retrieved a folded sheet of paper from his jacket pocket and gave it to Sharon. "Several influential members of the church have organized a campaign to support replacing *The Pearl of Great Value* window with a different parable."

Daniel chuckled. "Ironically, now may be the perfect time for me to sermonize about the parable. With so many worshipers trying to figure out what it means, I'd have a sanctuary full of interested listeners and fewer people nodding off."

Sharon responded to Daniel's gentle quip with a weak smile—all the gaiety she could muster now that her mind had focused on another complaint in the critical e-mail. She decided to read the words aloud: "'The decision to keep or replace the parable should be made by church elders and members alone. We think it was a serious mistake for the Window Restoration Committee to bring in an outside consultant to tell us what to do.'"

Sharon exhaled slowly and went on. "I can sympathize with their desire to replace the parable, but the critics of the old window—as I'll call them—are plain wrong to blast Andrew Ballantine. The WinReC wanted expert advice to help us propose a solution to the elders. We never intended that Andrew would make the decision for the church."

"Perhaps not—but he expressed himself fairly strongly at the elders' special meeting. Many people in the pews came away thinking that Andrew spoke for the WinReC."

"That's almost funny," she said. "Ask Andrew how he feels about that. And as for speaking strongly, the poor man left the hospital the morning of the meeting. Instead of thanking him for showing up at all, the critics find fault with his inability to read people's minds. Nobody told him—or the WinReC— about the opposition to the old window."

Before Daniel could reply, the waitress arrived with their breakfasts. Sharon's SOGgy Benedict filled a whole plate. It consisted of an oversize English muffin, a circular slab of Canadian bacon, a thin omelet rather than the traditional poached eggs, and a hefty helping of Hollandaise sauce that looked and smelled homemade.

"If this is your 'usual' breakfast," she said, "I'm amazed that you don't weigh three hundred pounds."

"I eat breakfast here only once every other week," he said. "My *usual* breakfast is muesli and fruit. Lori's orders."

"You have a wise wife."

"I'll give thanks for her—and for our food."

After Daniel spoke a blessing, Sharon offered up her own silent prayer. *Lord, help me be patient. Help me listen. Guide me toward a decision that reflects Your will.*

Sharon tasted a small piece of her SOGgy Benedict. "Wow! It's delicious." She dove into the sandwich with vigor.

"You know, I'd like to add a PS to my blessing. Heavenly Father, please speed Andrew's healing.

"PPS," Sharon added. "Several days have gone by, but the

police still haven't discovered who poisoned Andrew. Please give Special Agent Keefe the information he needs to identify the person responsible. And give him the wisdom to stop thinking of me as a suspect."

Daniel's eyes opened wide. He rushed an "Amen!" then said, "You! The police think that you might have poisoned Andrew? That's absurd."

She nodded. "Unfortunately, it's not such a far-fetched idea. I made the Strathbogie Mist, I was with Andrew when he got sick, I know how to use the oleander toxin as a poison."

"Oh, my. I see your point."

"I haven't told anyone else, but I've started my own modest detecting effort."

"Do you know anything about detective work?"

"In a way, yes. People say that medical diagnoses is a kind of detecting. So I've begun to collect all the symptoms of the crime that happened on Sunday afternoon."

"I'm impressed. I think Lori would love that metaphor. *The symptoms of the crime.*"

"But you're not going to tell your wife, the police lieutenant, anything about my scheme…right?"

He laughed. "I wouldn't dare. But please be careful. I know from personal experience that dabbling in a criminal investigation can be dangerous."

"All I intend to do is keep my eyes open and gather a few facts."

Daniel groaned.

"I promise I'll be cautious," she said.

"It's not that." He sighed again. "The truth is, I'm not done telling you the troubling news."

He placed his fork neatly on his plate. "Rex Grainger, the editor of the *Glory Gazette,* heard about the intensified opposition to the old window. He announced to two of our elders that he plans to write an editorial for tomorrow's issue that argues the church must absolutely replace the window with a carbon copy—an exact duplicate."

Sharon outdid Daniel's earlier sigh. This was terrible news.

"What's his rationale?" she asked.

"That Glory Community Church's painted stained-glass windows are an integral part of the city's historic and artistic heritage."

"I am beginning to hate the word *heritage*."

Daniel signaled his agreement with a "Hmm." Then he said, "The editorial will also praise Andrew Ballantine's extraordinary wisdom and acumen, and urge the elders to play close attention to—and I quote Rex's words here—'a man of great wisdom who genuinely understands the vital contribution of *The Pearl of Great Value* window to Glory.'"

Sharon looked down at the remaining half of her SOGgy Benedict. No way would she be able to finish the enormous sandwich—not with her appetite plummeting because of Daniel's latest revelation. "Heaping praise on Andrew will infuriate everyone who dislikes the old window. It will achieve the opposite of what Rex Granger wants. Andrew will lose what little support he has left among Glory Community's decision makers."

"Even worse, Rex may be sowing the seeds for a nasty fight between the city and the church."

Sharon polished off the glass of orange juice that accompanied her breakfast and thought about Daniel's tentative prophecy. He was right. The citizens of Glory didn't care about the window's ability to teach, or the relative popularity of *The Pearl of Great Value* among parables at Glory Community

Church. Quite the contrary, their attention would be focused on the window's history and its impact on tourists. No doubt, they'd advocate duplicating the original Cottier illustration so that the restored window would match the image that tourists read about in the guidebooks.

But the elders were leaning in another direction. If city commissioners and Glory lawyers went to war over *The Pearl of Great Value*—and if the local newspaper continued to fan the flames of disagreement—the resulting quarrel would be long and messy.

Sharon poked listlessly at her SOGgy Benedict, then noticed that Daniel was doing the same thing to the remains of his sandwich. Moreover, he'd suddenly become distant—his eyes focused on his plate rather than her face.

An unpleasant thought filled her mind. "There's more 'troubling' news to come," she said. "You haven't told me everything."

His expression became somber as he nodded. "The critics, as you've dubbed them, have a final concern that they thankfully didn't include in the e-mail."

The discomfort Sharon heard in Daniel's voice could mean only one thing: they had launched a direct attack on her.

"What do they say I've done wrong?"

Daniel paused, apparently to choose the perfect words. "They asked me to find out if the chair of our Windows Restoration Committee is thinking for herself, or whether she's become wholly captivated by Andrew Ballantine."

Sharon flinched as if she'd been slapped.

"Daniel, let me assure you that my relationship with Andrew is completely open and professional."

"You don't have to assure me of anything, Sharon. Regrettably, a few people noticed the *affectionate* way you stared at Andrew when he spoke in the sanctuary on Tuesday night."

She felt her eyes grow wide. "I was *that* transparent?"

"'Fraid so." Daniel laughed. "But admiring an impressive man who's making a fine presentation is hardly a sin. I told them that. I also strongly recommended that they remove these kinds of personal attacks from their campaign."

Sharon voiced a growl-like grunt. "Chairing this committee was supposed to be a no-brainer—a simple matter of replacing a damaged window with an identical replica. I didn't anticipate a battle royal."

"Nor did I when I asked you to take the job. Do you want out?"

"I can't deny that I want my life back, but I made a promise to the church. I won't quit—no matter what."

"That's what I hoped you'd say." He patted her arm. "Glory Community needs someone to see this mess through to the bitter end. I'm sorry I chose you, but I'm also glad I did—if you understand what I mean."

She sipped her coffee then smiled at him. "I understand perfectly, Daniel."

Sharon said her goodbyes, unlocked her bicycle, and secured a paper bag holding the leftovers of her SOGgy Benedict to the rack behind her seat. She'd planned to pedal west on Oliver Street, south on Broad Street, then west on Main, but because a bright sun had warmed the morning, she decided to follow the scenic route to the hospital—a big circle around Glory that would take her alongside Albemarle Sound.

She didn't admit it to Daniel, but she was still smarting from the accusation that she'd been "captivated" by Andrew Ballantine. She shouldn't have been surprised by it, not in a small city like Glory, where people paid close attention to unintended glances and gazes. She'd been foolish to wear her heart on her face in the sanctuary.

Imagine if people knew how you feel about him now?

But her growing fondness for Andrew didn't have an impact upon the decisions she made. The "critics" wouldn't have insulted her integrity if they'd witnessed Andrew's reaction to her idea of compromise—and his coolness toward her last night.

The very word *captivate* had startled her when Daniel had spoken it. Being captivated was a small step away from falling in love. Her relationship with Andrew hadn't reached that point yet, and probably never would. If disagreements over the window didn't keep them apart, he'd doubtless run away when he learned about her failed marriage.

She turned right on the Glory Strand and accelerated, enjoying the sensation of speed. The wintery sun had risen high enough in the sky to make the chop on the Albemarle's surface sparkle. Glory in December might not look like a Christmas card, but Christmastime here could be enchanting nonetheless.

You have to do something about Andrew. Soon.

She heard her cell phone ringing and recalled she'd stowed it in her jacket pocket. She wheeled her bicycle onto the grassy strip between The Strand and Albemarle Sound and hopped off. The name on the phone's caller ID screen: Andrew Ballantine.

He must have read my mind.

"It's Andrew," he said. "I hope it's not too early to call you."

"Not at all." Her heart had begun to thump, seemingly for no reason. "I'm on my way to work."

"If I remember right, today is your half day."

"It is. I get off at noon."

"Well, I plan to visit an old friend of mine. I'd love you to come along with me."

"An old friend? Where?"

"In New Bern, North Carolina. I won't tell you any more now, but I promise you'll find her fascinating—and the visit worthwhile. I'll get box lunches for us." When she hesitated, he added, "Trust me. Say yes."

Be sensible. Say no.

Sharon stared at her phone. She had more important things to do with her free time during Christmas season than take pointless junkets to New Bern, with a confirmed bachelor who planned to return to Asheville.

"I'll meet you at The Scottish Captain at twelve-thirty."

"Terrific!"

She climbed back on her bicycle, flipped the chain into high gear, and wondered why she'd given in so easily.

Talk about a stupid question. Spending time with Andrew makes you happy.

She laughed as she stair-stepped the pedals and propelled herself down Main Street.

EIGHT

Andrew checked his watch. Twelve-fifteen. Too early to go downstairs and wait for Sharon. He used the time to order last-minute presents for his parents—a trout-fishing reel for his father, a set of imported cooking knives for his mother. He chuckled at the thought that both gifts might come in handy at the same time, if Mom prepared a fish that Dad caught.

Andrew chided himself at the end of every Christmas season when he totaled up the large sum he'd spend on over-night shipping. This year would be no different. Most of the people who knew him assumed that he was a model of efficiency. In fact, when it came to thinking about friends and family, he could be rather disconnected. He'd decided on the gifts months earlier, but had found reasons to postpone ordering them.

The wages of procrastination are hefty.

He bounded down the stairs and took up position in front of The Scottish Captain.

"We're not going to fight about the window today," Andrew said to the sidewalk, as if speaking the words aloud would make them true. "The church window brought us together. I won't let it rip us apart."

He checked his watch. Twelve twenty-five. Still early. And she might even be a few minutes late.

But what if she changes her mind and doesn't come?

He walked to his SUV parked near the entrance and leaned against the front fender. Andrew knew he was thinking like a lovesick teenager, but he couldn't shake his fear that Sharon would see through his confident facade and discover the flaws that made him a hard man to love. This very thing had destroyed his relationships with other women.

I won't let it happen with Sharon.

A flash of motion caught his eye. Possibly a curtain fluttering in the Captain's front window. He wondered if Emma was watching him, but then decided she had better things to do on a Thursday afternoon than observe one of her guests fretting foolishly on the sidewalk.

He heard a bell ring nearby. He looked right and spotted Sharon bicycling north on Broad Street. She waved and smiled. Her rosy cheeks and windswept hair proved she'd been hurrying. That, plus her obvious enthusiasm to see him drove away the last of his concerns.

This will be a wonderful day.

She was dressed in tan slacks, her brilliant red all-weather jacket, and an even brighter red scarf. She carried a gleaming green parcel under her left arm. The mix of vivid colors made her look like a golden-haired Christmas elf.

"This arrived for you at the hospital this morning." She hopped off her bike, swiveled the kickstand downward with her foot, and handed him the package.

Andrew deciphered the repeating patterns of letters embossed on the shimmering wrapping paper. "The Glory of Chocolate."

"The best chocolatier in North Carolina," she said. "Their handmade truffles are absolutely delicious." She touched the shipping label taped to the front of the package. "It's a gift from Michael and Haley Carroll. A messenger delivered it to the information kiosk in the Glory Regional's lobby. They must think you're still a patient."

He shrugged. "The Carrolls left the Captain early on Tuesday morning. I wanted to thank Dr. Haley for looking after me at the tea party, but never had the chance."

He hefted the package close to his ear and gave it a gentle shake. "It sounds like a one-pound box of chocolate truffles." He added. "A pound of truffles is scarcely enough for the two of us, but let's munch on them as we drive to our surprise destination."

Sharon refused to take the parcel from him when he tried to give it back to her. "Please don't bring them along. I love chocolate truffles and will devour them. I'll tell the world you're responsible when patients faint at the sight of my nose dotted with zits."

He made a face to counter hers. "I couldn't live with the guilt." He broke into a grin. "For the good of everyone who'll see you during Christmas season, we won't trifle with the truffles. You lock up your bike and I'll stash the candy inside the Captain." Andrew clambered up the front steps in a single bound and left the box of candy on a table in the foyer.

When he returned to the SUV, Sharon was sitting in the front seat. "Are you going to tell me who we're going to visit in New Bern? Or do you plan to keep it a secret until we get there?"

"This will be a day full of surprises." He started the engine. "Trust me, you'll like them all."

Andrew drove north on Broad Street, then left on Main. Rafe Neilson had provided the simplest, most direct route to

New Bern at breakfast. Pick up State Route 34A at the Glory city limits, continue to U.S. Route 17, then meander west and south to their destination. By one o'clock, they'd traveled twenty-five of the one hundred twenty-five miles.

"I believe it's time for lunch," he said.

"Lunch?" she frowned.

"Did I say something wrong? I told you last night that I'd bring a box lunch."

"I had a rather large breakfast this morning. I made sincere plans not to eat again for…at least a month or two."

He laughed. "In that event, break out *my* lunch. There's a bag on the backseat from the Glorious Gourmet. I bought non-drippy food we—I mean *I*—can eat with my fingers. Smoked turkey sandwiches on sourdough bread, bags of Hawaiian potato chips and cranberry cookies for dessert."

He glanced at Sharon; she was cheerfully browsing through the bag. "If you definitely don't want lunch," he said, "you'll also find bottles of flavored water and insulated mugs full of coffee."

"Here's your sandwich," she said after a while. "I put a bottle of water in your cup holder. Eat, drink—and keep your eyes on the road." Andrew heard the sound of sandwich paper crinkling in the passenger seat. "I never said that I 'definitely' don't want my sandwich," she said. "I pride myself on my flexibility. I'm willing to change even my most sincere plans when the circumstances require that I change."

"What circumstances are those?" he asked.

"I've never met a Glorious Gourmet sandwich I could resist."

Andrew accelerated to pass a slow-moving truck on Route 17. Sharon was definitely in a good mood this afternoon. Hooray for that. But then, he'd never seen her in a really bad mood. She always seemed able to maintain her buoyancy—even when he'd managed to make her angry. That was one of the things he found most attractive about her.

He gripped the steering wheel tightly and decided to take a risk. "May I ask a personal question?" he said. "You can tell me to keep my ears on the road if it annoys you."

"Do I have to stop eating my turkey sandwich?"

"Feel free to talk with your mouth full."

"Then ask away." She spoke in a mumble.

"When and why did you move to Glory?"

She didn't respond for several seconds. He'd begun to wonder if she would when she said, "The 'when' was last January. As for 'why'—I'd lived in Charlotte for a dozen years and decided to try a smaller city clear across the state from my ex-husband."

Andrew listened intently to the tone of her voice. She didn't seem to mind sharing her history. If anything, she sounded relieved, although he couldn't imagine the reason.

He was about to ask the obvious next question when Sharon continued on her own. "I expect that you're wondering about my divorce, so I'll tell you the rest of my sad tale." She began with a sigh. "My husband found another woman he preferred to me. It's not a pretty story…"

He completed her sentence. "But it's a common one."

"And much more painful than people who haven't been there realize. First, you feel stupid that you trusted a spouse who betrayed you. Second, you become bitter—wary of trusting anyone again."

"And third, you move ahead with your life," he said.

"Perhaps," she said softly. "If you're willing to take the risk of trusting someone else." She abruptly sat up in her seat. "So much for my nuptial history—what about yours?"

"I don't have a history. I never married."

"You told me at the tea party that you're a confirmed bachelor, that you're resigned to being single. Is that because you never found the right woman?"

"Well, I thought I had on a couple of occasions, but whatever attraction we shared soon evaporated. Something about me gets in the way of solid relationships." He turned his head and caught a glimpse of her. She seemed absorbed by his confession. "You may find this hard to believe, but some women say that I'm too wrapped up in my work—that I'm fanatical about stained glass. One gal called me a single-minded workaholic."

"Ouch! How could anyone even suggest that about you?" She tossed in a sarcastic whistle to further poke fun at him. "What a silly idea, considering how little you've accomplished in your career."

"I'm not as career-obsessed as I used to be. The truth is I've mellowed over the years."

"I doubt that. It's hard to think of you ripening like a well-aged cheese and losing your passion for church windows."

"Okay, then maybe I've grown a bit wiser with each passing year."

As the miles ticked by, Andrew noted that their conversation shifted toward small talk. They talked about their Scotties… about the virtues of different kinds of bicycles…and about the joys of attending graduate school in England. Almost by mutual consent, neither he nor Sharon brought up stained-glass windows or the police investigation.

Good. Neither of us wants to argue today.

Every time Andrew smiled at Sharon, she returned his smile. Another good sign. If they could maintain their affability, they might eventually recover the intimacy they'd enjoyed at the tea party.

"We're here," Sharon said excitedly. "We just passed the Entering New Bern sign. It's time for you to fess up."

"We're going to visit an old friend of mine named Franny Brewer. She owns the New Bern Glass Workshop. I consider Franny the best stained-glass designer and craftsman in the Carolinas. I know you'll find her studio fascinating."

He cast a glance at Sharon and saw a small frown appear around her eyes then quickly vanish.

"A stained-glass studio…" She left the question hanging.

"Remember my promise. All surprises will be pleasant ones."

Route 17 made a sweeping right turn and became a mile-long bridge across the Neuse River. Andrew steered the SUV to the right side of road and took the exit that led to the smaller drawbridge over the Trent River—and into downtown New Bern. He drove along East Front Street, past Union Point Park on the right and the Craven County Convention Center on the left. The low December sun seemed to perch directly above the taller buildings and church steeples.

"What a pretty little city," Sharon said. "I've never been to New Bern before."

"Swiss settlers founded the town in 1710. New Bern was North Carolina's first state capital."

Andrew turned left on Pollock Street. "The glass workshop is coming up on the right. Look for a cool stained-glass sign. It sparkles in the daylight."

"I see it. One block ahead."

"Franny runs a top-notch glass studio. She's blended traditional craftsmanship with computerized equipment that automates stained-glass development and manufacture. I know that

Glory Community Church will get competitive bids to build the replacement window, but I hope that Franny wins."

"Isn't it a tad early to talk about building our window?"

Andrew had anticipated the hint of anxiety he heard in her voice. "*Much* too early," he said, doing his best to blend friendliness with irony. "Therefore—remember my promise."

"You keep saying that."

"Only because you keep forgetting." He steered the SUV into the workshop's small parking lot.

He made a show of scooting around the SUV and opening the door for her. "You will like all surprises today." She rolled her eyes but seemed amused by his unpredictability. He escorted Sharon to the front door.

Franny Brewer was a short, good-looking brunette in her mid-forties, with remarkably big brown eyes that seemed even larger behind the oversize glasses she wore. She immediately gave Andrew a massive hug.

"You ungrateful man! It's high time you came to see me, considering the number of times I've saved your bacon at the last moment." She pushed him away. "You must be Sharon Pickard. Welcome to my studio. How much did Andrew tell you about what he asked me to do?"

"Absolutely nothing."

"True," Andrew said. "I wanted to surprise her."

"Then that's what we'll do." Franny took Sharon's hand. "Follow me."

Andrew trailed behind as Franny shepherded Sharon past a heavy industrial double door into a large high-ceilinged workshop. "We build our windows in here. The first step in fabricating anything out of stained glass is to cut the glass into appropriately shaped pieces. We do that three different ways—

When we need pieces of glass in simple, straight or curved shapes, we use a traditional handheld glass cutter or our new computer-controlled glass-cutting machine. For small, odd-shaped pieces, we use our band-saw equipped with a diamond-coated glass-cutting blade."

Franny guided them to a wood-topped workbench. A lanky mustachioed man holding a smoking soldering iron in his left hand and a spool of solder in his right hovered over a rectangular glass panel.

"A large church window consists of several panels like this one," Franny explained. "The individual pieces of stained glass are held together with *came*—thin lead bars with channels on each side. The ends of the cames are soldered together to assemble each window panel. Then we apply putty to fill the remaining space between the glass and the channels. The process is called leading-up."

Franny pointed to an object that looked like a garbage can made of white bricks. "That's a glass kiln—a custom-made electric oven. Many of our glass pieces are painted after they're cut. We fire them at a temperature of about nine hundred degrees Fahrenheit to fuse the paint to the glass surface."

Andrew watched Sharon walk around the workshop and look at window panels in different stages of assembly. She seemed interested, but would she ever care as much about stained glass as he did?

"That's the wrong question," he muttered to himself. Only one thing really mattered. Would she care about him as much as he cared about her?

Franny pointed toward an office area at the back of the workshop. "Of course, every stained-glass window begins with a cartoon."

Sharon brightened. "Andrew talked about cartoons. They're full-size drawings of stained-glass panels."

"We used to hand-draw cartoons on paper. But now that we're computerized, we can print the cut lines directly on sheets of stained glass." Franny sat down in front of an oversize monitor and tapped the keyboard to wake up the computer. "But the most exciting benefit of the new technology is that we can preview stained-glass windows before we build them." She pressed several keys.

"Wow!" Sharon exclaimed. "That's *The Pearl of Great Value* window."

"I sent Franny the digital files of Lori Hartman's photographs," Andrew said.

"And I transformed them into cartoons that are almost as good as Daniel Cottier's original designs." Franny chuckled. "Now the magic begins. Here's an alternative window based on the parable of *The Wise and Foolish Virgins.*"

"The story is told in Matthew 25," Andrew said. "The five maidens who had prepared for the arrival of the bridegroom received rewards, while the five maidens who weren't prepared lost everything. Jesus linked this story to his Second Coming. It cautions us to be prepared for his return."

"The illustration matches our missing window perfectly," Sharon said.

"I tweaked an existing cartoon to make it more like Cottier's style, then I copied the color and glass palettes from Glory Community's other windows."

Sharon peered uncertainly at Andrew. He replied with a big grin. "I'm not stupid. I know that the elders will probably decide not to replace *The Pearl of Great Value* window."

Sharon's stare grew more intense. He made a vague gesture

of surrender. "I told the elders that matching the other windows would be difficult—I didn't say it was impossible."

Andrew had planned much of the morning what he would say next. It flowed off his tongue in a single burst. "You wanted compromise. Well, here it is. If the elders want a new window, I'll work closely with them to identify a parable that ties in with the surviving windows. Then I'll work closely with an appropriate stained-glass artist to create a cartoon that harmonizes with Cottier's original designs."

Sharon smiled at him. Well, if truth be told, she beamed at him. No other word described the joy in her expression. Perhaps now he could dare to believe that she'd forgiven his gaffe in the hospital cafeteria.

Franny pressed more keys, restoring the image of the old window. "Actually, it's time for a change," she said, "this is far from Cottier's best church window."

Andrew didn't intend to groan, but it slipped out. "Not you, too, Franny."

"I call 'em like I see 'em." She laughed. "Cottier made *The Pearl of Great Value* look like a baseball. All that's missing is painted red stitching."

When Sharon snorted, Andrew fought to maintain his calm. He had no intention of cackling along with the ladies.

"On that silly note," he said, "we'll be off. It's a long trip back to Glory."

"Thanks for the lesson," Sharon said to Franny. "You've been a wonderful teacher. I've learned a lot this afternoon."

"Before you go," Franny said, "I want to thank you for the free publicity. A reporter at the *Glory Gazette* called and said that you mentioned my name."

"The paper's editor interviewed me yesterday," Andrew

explained. "One of his questions was about the stained-glass infrastructure in North Carolina. Naturally, I told him about you."

"Rex Grainger interviewed you?" Sharon asked. "I didn't know that."

"No big deal. He had a few technical questions about stained glass—so I answered them." He recalled the telephone call. Rex had asked a dozen sensible questions and he had provided a dozen equally sensible answers. He felt proud of his performance.

Curiously, Sharon had raised the subject of Rex Grainger again as they drove north on Route 17 after stopping for a quick fast-food supper. "Did he want your opinions about replacing the original window?"

"Not really. He seemed to understand how I feel about historic and artistic integrity."

"Oh, boy."

"What does that mean?"

"Nothing. I'm only blithering."

She hesitated then said, "Did Rex ask you any questions about your poisoning?"

"Nope. The story seems to have died down. Reporters don't care anymore and I haven't heard anything from the police, either. It's almost as if everyone wants to forget about the…ah, unpleasant incident at The Scottish Captain. I'd certainly like to think it was all a big accident."

"If only that were true."

Sharon settled into her seat and closed her eyes. In a minute or two her quiet breathing signaled that she'd fallen asleep.

He glanced at her. She looked like an angel.

My angel.

NINE

Sharon had meant to stay alert, watch the road and keep Andrew company during the long-slow drive to Glory on Route 17, but after they dined on burgers in Washington, North Carolina, her mind filled with a hodgepodge of happy thoughts about the things he'd done that day to please her.

Andrew had devised an elaborate outing that succeeded brilliantly. She'd been skeptical when they'd arrived at the stained-glass workshop, but she left delighted with all that Franny Brewer had shown her.

Much more important, Andrew had brought about a sea change in his attitude that truly reflected his willingness to compromise. He admitted that he still preferred the original window, but how could anyone expect anything different from a man of his determination? Despite his preference, Andrew would help the elders find a proper replacement if they chose not to duplicate *The Pearl of Great Value*.

It couldn't have been easy for Andrew to adopt such a radical shift in his thinking, and she could think of only one explanation for his change of heart. Somehow, their growing relationship had prompted him to come up with an alternative strategy. Was this a sign that his affection for her had also increased?

Maybe…but don't rush ahead into unchartered territory.

The only sour note was Rex Granger. He'd evidently called Andrew for information to flesh out the editorial that would be published on Friday, but Sharon doubted that Rex had explained his purpose before he asked his questions. Andrew might not have been so cooperative if he'd known that Rex was a determined opponent to compromise.

Well, I'll find out tomorrow when I read the Gazette.

She leaned her head against the SUV's soft leather upholstery as the sun disappeared behind the trees and remembered that tomorrow would be the shortest day of the year, which happened three or four days before Christmas. When she was a child, she believed that Santa Clause began loading his sleigh when the winter solstice began….

The next thing she heard was the ratcheting noise of Andrew setting the hand brake, followed by "Rise and shine, Sleeping Beauty. We're back at the Captain."

Sharon blinked awake. It was dark outside, but the orange beam from a sodium-vapor streetlamp illuminated the interior of the SUV. Andrew was gazing at her, a contented grin on his face. He should be tired after so much solo driving, but he seemed chipper, in high spirits. She smiled back at him and stretched her arms behind the top of her seat.

"Thanks for a delightful afternoon," she said. "I'd better head home."

"Not so fast. We have to crack open the box of chocolate truffles before you go."

"I'd forgotten about your gift."

"Not me! Anticipating chocolate truffles made by the best chocolatier in North Carolina kept me alert for the last fifty miles."

"Goodness! Now I feel thoroughly guilty for napping. You should have woken me."

"The only way you can make it up to me is by eating your fair share of the goodies—and let your pristine nose fend for itself."

"You're a hard man, Andrew Ballantine."

She slipped out of her seat an instant before The Scottish Captain's porch light flashed on. Amanda Turner stepped out the front door towing a small wheeled suitcase. Emma followed close behind with a larger wheeled bag.

Amanda's eyes began to blaze when she saw Andrew standing next to his SUV. "Dr. Ballantine," she purred, "I'm so glad that you're back. It would have been awful to leave without saying goodbye. I worried that you'd drive home to Asheville and forget about me." She spotted Sharon. "And it's delightful to see you again, too, Sharon."

"Amanda is returning to The Robert Burns Inn," Emma said. "The renovations are nearly finished."

Amanda nodded. "My contractor called with the blessed news this afternoon. The last of the carpet is down and all but two guest bathrooms have been painted and repapered. I can go home—although the Bobby Burns is scarcely that, yet. I've only spent three nights there. Thanks to Emma's wonderful hospitality, I think of the Captain as more of a home than my own B and B."

She turned her attention fully on Andrew. "However, because my little establishment is now open for business, I decided to throw a before-church reception on Christmas Eve. It's my little way of repaying the friendliness I've experienced during the past week. Emma has agreed to come and bring her delightful husband. Please tell me that you'll join me for canapés and Christmas punch." She smiled at Sharon. "And you, too, of course."

Andrew heaved an unhappy sigh. "Thank you, Amanda. I'll do my best to be there."

"I certainly hope so, darlin'," she drawled. "We've become such good friends during my stay here."

Good friends? The words upset Sharon because of the coy tone of voice that Amanda applied and the unmistakable come-hither look in her eyes. The woman was flirting with Andrew—in a way that suggested she'd done it before.

Sharon felt her own eyes narrow. For a giddy instant she wondered if her nails were sharp enough to claw Amanda's face off. And then her commonsensical mind took over.

It takes two to play the dating game.

She looked at Andrew. Even bathed in orange light, his face burned red with anger. Amanda might've been pitching, but Andrew wasn't catching.

Amanda gave Emma a bear-sized goodbye embrace then rolled her suitcases down the ramp that paralleled the Captain's front steps. Sharon guessed that Amanda hoped that Andrew would help carry her clobber to the parking lot, but before he could react, Emma took charge of the big suitcase again and led Amanda around the side of the building.

Andrew waited until Amanda was out of earshot to say, "I'm tempted to put her image in a stained-glass window—just so I can toss a rock at it."

Sharon laughed. "Now I know why you spent so much time away from the Captain."

Emma returned to the front of the B and B and pointed her finger at Andrew: "Don't blame Amanda. It's your fault for being so good-looking."

"I agree. It's a curse." He smirked, then trod up the steps and into the Captain.

Sharon groaned. "Unwrap those chocolates before I toss a rock at you."

An instant later, Andrew said, "It's gone. I put the package on the table in the hallway after lunch. But now the table's empty."

"A green parcel—from The Glory of Chocolate?" Emma asked.

"That's the one."

"I stashed it in the kitchen for safekeeping." She cocked her thumb in the kitchen's direction. "And mostly to lead me not into temptation." She added, "I'll meet you in the front parlor. Does anyone else want a glass of milk?"

Sharon said, "Yes, please," and Andrew agreed.

She walked with Andrew into the front parlor and came to a halt in the entranceway. Emma had finished decorating the parlor's Christmas tree, the largest of the Captain's four trees. The ornaments were simple glass spheres, but the profusion of colors and surface textures created a spectacular sight.

"One look at that tree and I want to sing Christmas carols," Andrew said from behind her. "Although my singing voice would definitely put a damper on the season."

She laughed and led him into the parlor. They chose the sofa that had the largest coffee table. When he sat down next to her, she said, "I haven't had a chance to thank you, but I appreciate the compromise you came up with. You've made it much easier for the WinReC to finish up its work." She meet his eyes. "Do you think Franny Brewer might be willing to lend us the computerized image of the alternative window? I'd love to show it to the elders, so they can understand what's possible."

He grinned and reached into his pocket.

"Ta-da!" He gave her a flash drive key fob. "Now playing

at a computer near you—everything you saw on Franny's big monitor."

"I feel like hugging you."

"Don't let me stop you," Emma said. She sat alongside Sharon and set a tray down on the coffee table: A jug of milk. Three glasses. Napkins. The wrapped box of chocolates.

Sharon smiled at Andrew when he picked up the package. "I hope you intend to send the Carrolls a thank-you note," she said. "Haley and Michael have been extremely generous. The Glory of Chocolate is one of our priciest specialty shops. A box of truffles that big costs as much as dinner for two at The Glorious Table."

"Very generous," he agreed, "considering that the Carrolls hardly know me. I never said anything other than hello to either of them."

Sharon wasn't surprised. She had often been pleasantly surprised by the kindness she'd received from small-town physicians. The Carrolls hailed from Wilson, a city not much larger than Glory. Big-city doctors might have a reputation for being arrogant, at times indifferent, but the local doctors she'd worked with at Glory Regional Hospital had been caring, supportive—and generous.

Andrew positioned the package on his lap. "To quote Macbeth 'it were well it were done quickly.'" He tore the wrapping paper off in one continuous motion, then crumpled it into a ball.

"Just like a man," Emma said. She smoothed the rumpled paper and folded it into a rectangle. "It's easier to recycle this way."

Andrew lifted the green lid and the gilded paper candy pad. "Rats! They aren't truffles. These are cordial cherries."

"I'm confident we'll muddle through," she said. "I love chocolate cherries."

"By all means—ladies first." He offered the box to Sharon. She plucked a cordial cherry out of the center of the box.

"Don't eat it!" Emma shouted slapping Sharon's fingers. The chocolate cherry went flying across the parlor and landed on a side table. She yanked the candy box out of Andrew's hand and laid it on the coffee table.

Sharon stared at Emma, wondering how to respond to her bizarre behavior.

"I haven't gone crazy," Emma said. "Look at the label on the wrapping paper."

Sharon peered at the folded paper rectangle. The label was visible on the top layer. She read aloud: "To Dr. Andrew Ballantine from Mr. and Mrs. Michael Carroll." She glanced at Andrew; he looked as bewildered as she was by Emma's rationale.

"Don't you get it?" Emma said. "Haley Carroll is a physician, and proud of it. She identified herself as Dr. Carroll when she made reservations. She called herself Dr. Carroll when she checked in last Sunday. She introduced herself as Dr. Haley Carroll at the tea party. I can't imagine her settling for 'Mrs. Michael Carroll' on an expensive gift she sent to *Dr.* Andrew Ballantine."

Sharon studied the paper debris more carefully. "But what if she ordered the candy by telephone and a salesperson filled out the label?"

"That's a possibility…" Emma admitted. "But where's the cellophane? Every other box of candy I've seen from The Glory of Chocolate came with a cellophane wrapper around the box."

Sharon thought about it; Emma was right. She took another cherry cordial out of the box and examined it. "Oh my! I can see a tiny hole in the side, near the bottom. A tiny bit of cordial filling has oozed out." She examined a second candy. "This one has a hole, too."

"In police speak," Emma said, "someone has tampered with these chocolates."

"Tampered with…as in *poisoned?*" Andrew asked softly.

Emma stood up. "I'm going to call Rafe. He's working late tonight."

The room fell silent. Sharon could hear the clock on the mantelpiece ticking. Sudden recognition stole her breath. *She had almost eaten a poisoned chocolate.* Her heart started to pound, she felt her eyes roll back in her head, and then everything went black.

"What happened?" she heard herself say, with what seemed her next breath.

"You had another Sleeping Beauty moment," Andrew replied. "This one snuck up on you unexpectedly."

When she opened her eyes, she realized she was lying on the sofa and that Emma was pressing a wet cloth against the back of her neck. She saw Andrew crouched alongside her and Rafe Neilson standing behind him.

"You're saying I fainted, Andrew. But that doesn't make any sense. I'm a nurse."

"A very lucky nurse," Rafe held out his hand. He wore a latex glove and held a smashed chocolate cherry. "Here's the candy you almost ate. The cordial interior seems much runnier than it should be."

"More oleander extract?"

"That's my guess. Injected into the chocolates through the holes you discovered. I'll ship the candies to NCSBI's forensic lab in the morning."

She thrust against the sofa and twisted herself into a sitting position. "I still feel wobbly. This is ridiculous and embarrassing. What kind of E.R. nurse passes out at the thought of eating tainted chocolate?"

"The sensibly fearful kind." Andrew patted her hand. "Your secret's safe with me."

"I'd better get home, to bed."

"Everyone agrees with you," Andrew said. "But you're not going to ride a bicycle tonight—not after the shock you've had."

"I'm feeling fine."

"You look fine, too. But I'm stubborn—and determined to drive you and your bicycle to Queen Street."

Sharon couldn't help giggling. Andrew had paraphrased the words she'd spoken a few days earlier, when he'd said the same thing.

"What time is it?"

"A few minutes past eight. Why?"

"This may sound crazy, but my mouth's still in the mood for chocolate—my favorite comfort food. All the stores that sell The Glory of Chocolate products are closed."

Emma laughed. "One of Calvin Constable's triple-chocolate brownies should tide you over until tomorrow. Would you like one, too, Andrew?"

He shook his head. "Thanks. But I've decided to give up sweets until Rafe and his colleagues catch whoever's responsible for…" He pointed at the candy box. "Oleander toxin is supposed to be bitter. I don't think it's an accident that the poisoner used Strathbogie Mist and cordial cherries to disguise the bad taste."

"Another fact you learned on the Internet?" Sharon said, feeling silly that she hadn't made the obvious connection between bitter and sweet. A spoonful of sugar helps the toxin go down.

Andrew winked at Sharon. "I searched on Wednesday."

Emma jumped in: "I hope you don't think that Calvin Constable might be the person responsible."

Rafe responded first. "Andrew didn't say that. The point—which I admit I overlooked—is that you need to hide the taste of Oleander toxin to get someone to consume it."

Sharon decided that this was a perfect time to leave. She stood and found—praise God—that she wasn't the least bit shaky. She bid farewells to Emma and Rafe, received her chocolate brownie in return, departed the Captain, and hefted her bike in place on the SUV's rear rack.

She zipped her jacket shut against the chill wind and wished she'd worn her heavier down-filled parka. The cloudless December sky had encouraged a rapid drop in temperature. Thank goodness she didn't have to pedal across Glory. The thought made her shiver.

When Andrew beeped the driver and passenger doors open, he said, "I promised you a day full of surprises. You can't say that I didn't deliver." He climbed inside and started the engine.

"You also assured me that I'd like all of them. I draw the line at poisoned chocolate cherries."

He reached over and secured her seat belt. "The day's not over. There's more than enough time for another pleasant surprise."

Sharon couldn't imagine anything she wanted less. She yearned to end the day by taking Heather for a short walk, then curling up with a mystery novel—one she'd read before.

This day has had more than enough unexpected twists.

Andrew parked in front of her town house. She stood behind the SUV, waiting for him to retrieve her bicycle, when he unexpectedly nudged her left shoulder and turned her around.

Then he put his arms around her, drew her close to him and lowered his lips on hers.

Sharon tightened her arms around Andrew and kissed him back—enjoying the tingles of electricity that flowed from her head to her toes. She realized with complete clarity that this wasn't a surprise. She'd known all along how Andrew felt about her.

He clung to her for a few seconds more, then gently pulled away. "Sharon. I wanted to do that almost from the moment I began to talk to you at the tea party. You're the most intriguing woman I've met in years."

She'd imagined him kissing her, but now that he had, she was tongue-tied—with no clever answer to give. She pulled his head toward hers, kissed him again, and managed to say, "I feel the same way about you, too, Andrew."

He embraced her again. "You're trembling."

"It's freezing out here."

He laughed. "And I stupidly thought it was me." He hugged her tighter. "I'll call you tomorrow…" It was a statement. A question. A promise.

She stood near her front door and watched him drive away. How foolish she'd been to worry about a church window. Who could care about colored glass and lead when someone wanted to kill Andrew Ballantine?

When she trembled again, she knew that the cold wasn't the cause.

TEN

Andrew woke up at first light on Friday morning after a restless night, elated that his life had changed, but also vaguely apprehensive about the future. He'd been tempted to blame these negative feelings on his rusty relationship machinery. After all, last night marked the first time in five years that he'd confessed his feelings to a woman.

But Andrew soon realized that none of the common pop-psychology clichés explained the anxiety that caromed around his consciousness. He wasn't having second thoughts now that he'd declared his feelings for Sharon. He didn't have cold feet or "buyer's remorse."

You're not afraid of keeping her—you're worried that you might lose her.

He peered out his window at Broad Street. There was a remote possibility—that she would bicycle to work along Broad Street, and that he'd catch a glimpse of her beautiful face. He quickly began to feel foolish. The only thing his watchfulness had accomplished was to make him wonder where Sharon was this morning, and what she was doing.

He thought about dialing her cell phone, perhaps even inviting her to lunch, but concluded that would make him seem clingy or needy. Sharon might become angry with him. Or worse yet, disillusioned with their new attachment.

Relationships could fail in a thousand different ways. His past failed liaisons proved the point. After a promising beginning, something unexpected would start the disenchantment ball rolling. Often something related to stained glass. "You put your career ahead of me." "You travel too much and are gone too long."

"Sharon Pickard will be different," he murmured. "I'll stay in love with her…she'll stay in love with me.

"Really?" he replied to himself. "How do you intend to accomplish that magic trick?"

He hadn't thought it through, but he knew one thing for sure. He couldn't go on ditching his own deeply held values to keep Sharon happy. That was a surefire route to disaster, because both of them would eventually end up miserable.

He turned on his laptop computer and arranged two windows side by side: *The Pearl of Great Value* on the left and Franny Brewer's *The Lost Coin* on the right. The differences were easy to spot, even in the small images on a laptop screen. He'd known Franny for more than a decade. She had the talent to create competent windows, but she wasn't in the same league as Daniel Cottier. She'd duplicated Cottier's color palette and imitated the general style of his cartoons, but never in a thousand years of trying would she capture the liveliness of Cottier's finished windows or their unmistakable sense of elegance.

Andrew slammed the laptop's lid shut and cursed his decision to propose a "compromise." The great-great-great-grandson of James Ballantine had taken the easy way out, abandoned *The Pearl of Great Value* window, and consigned a historic piece of art to oblivion.

He'd pleased Sharon in the short run, but what of the long-term impact to their relationship? Did Sharon really want him to forsake his integrity without a fight? Could she continue to respect a man who walked away from his principles, a man who abandoned the things he believed in?

Not when she took the time to think about the true cost of compromise.

Fortunately, he'd left himself an escape hatch. He'd told Sharon that "if the elders want a new window," he'd help them find one.

"*If* is a delightful word," he muttered.

Sharon presumed that the elders had reached a decision. In fact, they hadn't, which meant that he could still influence the design of the replacement window.

He'd have to be clever about it, of course. No more frontal attacks in open meetings. He'd worked with enough churches to know how elder boards operated. Few elders took the time to become knowledgeable about every issue the church faced. Rather, the majority would defer to the one elder who everyone recognized as the expert—and go along with his decision.

For some reason, Gregory "Greg" Grimes had taken the lead on replacing the window. At Tuesday's meeting, he purported to speak for the rest of the elder board—and the general membership, to boot.

Andrew felt confident that Greg was the key, the advocate he needed to save *The Pearl of Great Value.* If he could win Grimes over, change his opinions about discarding the original window, Greg would exercise his influence on the other elders. Grimes was the only person in Glory who could do the job.

Andrew waited until nine-thirty to visit Greg. He decided to show up unannounced. Why give the man a chance to say no?

Andrew's GPS system lead him to a large Victorian house

on Princess Street, a hundred feet north of Stewart Lane. The house was tall enough to give the rooms on the third floor excellent views of Albemarle Sound. Andrew was startled to see a stained-glass suncatcher hanging in every front window—each one a colorful image of a different bird. The effect was attention-grabbing, if a bit garish.

Greg answered the door on Andrew's first push of the button.

"Dr. Ballantine…" He stared up at Andrew, plainly mystified to see him.

Andrew guessed that Greg Grimes was in his early sixties. A visit to Glory Community Church's Web site had yielded a brief biography: He was a retired social studies teacher, who'd also coached Glory High School's debating team. No wonder Grimes had framed a tough argument the other evening. In daylight, the man had striking gray eyes—or were they green?

"Would you have a moment, sir? I'd like to chat."

Greg hesitated. "Okay, we can chat—after I show you something that you might find interesting."

He led Andrew into a spotless foyer, down an equally spotless hallway, to a sparkling kitchen and into a small room—Andrew guessed it had once been a butler's pantry—that had been converted into a compact workshop. He immediately recognized a complete assortment of cutters, pliers and soldering tools used to build stained-glass objects.

"Stained glass has been my hobby for ten years." Greg sat down at his workbench. "I'm working on my biggest project now. Six panels that I'll mount in a wooden frame to create a room-divider screen for our bedroom. I've finished three of them and I'm assembling number four."

Andrew looked over Greg's shoulder at the panels leaning against the wall behind his workbench. They depicted an aviary's worth of different birds in stylized woodland settings. The retired teacher had become an adept practitioner of the stained-glass-assembly technique attributed to the great Tiffany.

"I was going to invite you to look at my work," Greg said, "but I figured you'd tell me to get lost." He waived a small triangle of crimson red cathedral glass, transparent and perfectly colored. It seemed destined to become part of a bird's tail. "As you can see, I know a thing or two about stained glass." He spoke with pride and clearly wanted Andrew to compliment his latest creation.

"Very attractive," Andrew said. "A handsome example of decorative stained glass." There wasn't much else he could say. Greg had applied considerable skill to build the panels, but he had started with commercial, stained-glass cartoons—probably out of an inexpensive pattern book. By no stretch of the imagination could the humdrum designs be considered artworks. Mediocre cartoons led to mediocre glass projects. His finished screen would never be worth looking at.

No wonder Greg Grimes was willing to sacrifice *The Pearl of Great Value* window. The aesthetic sensibilities of Greg were one notch up from a "paint by numbers" projecteer.

Greg rotated his swivel chair and leaned back to faced Andrew. "What can I do for you this fine morning?"

There was another chair in the room, but Greg hadn't invited Andrew to sit down, so he dove in without any kind of pre-amble. "I'd like you to reconsider your position on the church's replacement window."

"Why would I do that?"

"Because duplicating the original window is the right thing to do."

"So you don't buy the contention that our windows are supposed to educate our members?"

"Not really. Church windows built centuries ago when people couldn't read the Bible had to do that. The windows in Glory Community Church are chiefly decorative and inspirational—particularly windows that Scripture-savvy churchgoers see over and over again every time they enter the sanctuary."

"Fascinating! Did you get that argument from Rex Grainger?"

"No. If anything, I mentioned it to him."

"When did you start collaborating with Rex?"

Greg's eyes, which now looked pale blue, converged on Andrew's face with an authority that made him feel uneasy. He could imagine those see-everything eyes skewering hundreds of high school debaters over the years.

"We're hardly collaborating," Andrew replied quickly. "Rex is writing an article about my work with the WinReC. He called me the other day with several questions about the old window and about how stained-glass panels are assembled. Rex told me that the piece will be published in today's edition."

Andrew decided he'd given enough of an answer. Greg would find out soon enough that the editor of the *Glory Gazette* was a solid supporter of the *old-window* camp—a committed advocate of duplicating *The Pearl of Great Value.*

Greg held his piece of red glass up to the light that illuminated his workbench. "You know, I'd accept your position in an instant if all we had to do was replace a few pieces of glass. We'd try our best to duplicate the original color and texture. But I do not agree with your assertion that we have a responsibility to reproduce a window that's been totally destroyed."

Andrew swallowed his frustration. It began to dawn on him that Greg was in no mood for Andrew to try to get him to see the situation from his perspective.

Greg frowned at Andrew. "Glory was hit by Hurricane Gilda last summer. If the city had been a bit less lucky, our whole church might have been knocked down, instead of merely our steeple. I was one of the church members who helped to hang wooden storm shutters to protect our stained-glass windows. Contrary to what you think about me, I believe they represent an asset to both the church and Glory." His eyes drilled into Andrew once again. "Did Sharon Pickard suggest that you try to change my mind?"

"No."

"Good. Because it's up to the elders, not the WinReC, to reach a final decision"

"I agree completely, but you need good counsel to reach the right decision. The WinReC hired me to provide that."

"Maybe so, but do you really think you know us well enough to provide useful advice? I grant that you know our windows. But…you don't know much about our church. You don't understand our traditions. You don't appreciate our members' needs. You don't know our theology—or anything about us as people." He laughed, this time mockingly. "In other words, you're a typical consultant."

Andrew ignored the insult. "I was hired to consult, but my chief concern is the artistic and historic heritage that exists within Glory Community Church. I don't believe that the majority of church members are eager to abandon *The Pearl of Great Value* window."

"That's where you're wrong, Dr. Ballantine. Most of our members hate the old window. During the past two days, I've received upwards of a hundred e-mails urging the elders to commission a new design."

Andrew hid his surprise. "People are sending e-mails?"

"Indeed they are. The window has become a source of contention within the church—thanks largely to you."

Greg's fresh burst of hostility irritated Andrew, but he bit his tongue. Better to give the elder a full opportunity to vent.

Greg's frown deepened. "Let me tell you this, Dr. Ballantine. When the elder board makes decisions, we do our best to accommodate the wishes of church members. We'll listen to suggestions from experts like you, but we don't feel bound to follow them. That's especially true when we see a fight looming on the horizon. The unity of Glory Community Church is more important than a stained-glass window in our sanctuary. Do I make myself clear?"

Andrew nodded slowly. The elder had proved to be an unmovable object and there wasn't anything more Andrew could do to soften his intransigence. He'd lost the battle, but he didn't have to lose his dignity.

"I enjoyed talking with you," Andrew said, "even though I don't agree with your position on the window restoration."

Greg's frown didn't soften as he led Andrew to the front door. "Goodbye, Dr. Ballantine. Thank you for your concern. Rest assured that the elders will do the right thing."

Andrew thought about Greg's "assurance" as he started his SUV. The elders didn't have the know-how to do the right thing. That left Plan B, the compromise he'd promised Sharon. He'd do his best locate an acceptable artist. Without his help, Glory Community Church would end up with a third-rate window.

And the church might not care today, but in the future they'd come to regret their hasty decision.

ELEVEN

Sharon agreed to follow doctor's orders.

Ken Lehman had sidled next to her and said, "We've got everyone stabilized and admitted upstairs. Take a break and grab some breakfast."

"Thanks, boss. Yell if you need me."

Shortly after three in the morning, a driver had fallen asleep at the wheel and steered his minivan into the ditch on the side of State Route 34A. The paramedics transported him, his wife and his two kids to Glory Regional Hospital's Emergency Room a few minutes before four. Sharon had been called in to assist. Now at 10:00 a.m. she'd have a chance to eat the big breakfast she'd promised herself when she'd drifted off to sleep the night before.

She'd been too excited to eat after Andrew had astonished her with his unexpected kiss. He'd taken her breath away, and also her appetite. The day had been an emotional roller coaster for her. She'd soared high in New Bern because Andrew's compromise would let the elders make a quick decision—and terminate her WinReC responsibilities. Hours later, she'd plummeted to the depths of despair when the poisoner made a second attempt on Andrew's life. And then Andrew's kiss had rocketed her heart skyward with the promise that she wouldn't spend this Christmas alone after all.

But where was the roller coaster heading? What would she find at the end of the wild ride with Andrew? She was beginning to believe that she could trust him—but was that really the case? If she looked at their relationship objectively, she'd have to admit that she didn't know Andrew well enough to be confident about his fidelity. In the end, he might prove too good to be true—another man who would betray her when another "right woman" entered his life.

The cafeteria was nearly empty. Sharon ordered two sausage-and-egg burritos, a large orange juice and a jumbo coffee. She thought about calling Andrew and inviting him to join her—but he'd undoubtedly enjoyed a massive breakfast at The Scottish Captain. Perhaps she'd eat with him tomorrow. Emma Neilson would happily let her "crash" Saturday brunch.

She'd finished most of one burrito when someone behind her shoulder said, "Good morning, Sharon." She glanced up at the pretty face of Angie Ringgold, one of the town's two female police officers. Angie held a cup of coffee and a plastic spoon.

"Uh…can I join you?" Angie asked almost cautiously.

"Absolutely."

Angie sat down, added some half-and-half to her coffee, and gave a quick stir. Sharon noted an out-of-character red tinge on Angie's cheeks. Glory's utterly unflappable lady cop seemed embarrassed this morning.

"Would you like half of my second burrito?" Sharon said.

"No, I can't take time to eat. I'm here on…*business.*" Angie took a deep breath. "Special Agent Keefe wants to dialogue with you at Police Headquarters. At three o'clock this afternoon."

Sharon strove without much success to ignore the frisson of

fear that sent chills through her body. "Dialogue" was a curiously informal word for a detective to use when he issued an invitation. She was also surprised that Keefe had sent Angie Ringgold to summon her. A simple telephone call would have sufficed.

"Did he say what this is about?"

Sharon knew she'd asked a silly question. Keefe wanted to talk to her about the poisoned chocolate cherries she gave to Andrew Ballantine. For the second time in five days, she was linked to food intended to kill him.

Poor Angie's face became even redder. She stared at her coffee spoon and said, "I'm supposed to tell you that the dialogue will last about thirty minutes."

"I understand."

"So you'll be there?"

Sharon nodded. "Tell Agent Keefe to expect me at three on the dot."

"Thank you." Angie picked up her coffee and walked away—without saying another word.

Sharon watched her leave and wondered if the time had come to find a lawyer who knew how to deal with Keefe more effectively than she did. She'd once taken comfort in Rafe's words that Keefe was smart and experienced. But five hours from now, he'd level his skills and expertise against her—at the end of a long day that had begun in the middle of the night. She pictured herself locked behind bars in the Albemarle District Jail charged with a crime she hadn't committed—all because she'd accidentally said the wrong thing to Special Agent Tyrone Keefe of the NCSBI.

She was about to eat another bite of her burrito when Melanie Luft, the floor-duty nurse who'd looked after Andrew, slipped into the chair that Angie had vacated.

"I figured you'd want to see this." Melanie unfolded a pristine copy of the *Glory Gazette*. "The Friday issue just arrived at the gift shop. The lead article is about the man who came in with oleander poisoning on Sunday."

The front page made Sharon gasp: It featured a large photograph of Andrew in a gallant pose outside Glory Community Church, gazing resolvedly at the missing stained-glass window. Directly above was a huge headline: *Stop the Murder of Glory's Artistic Legacy!*

"I don't believe it!" Sharon rose slowly to her feet. Her fears of Special Agent Tyrone Keefe seeped away like water soaking into sandy soil. "This time, *I'll* kill him!"

She stepped aside to let Melanie grab her newspaper and jog to a safer corner of the cafeteria.

At two forty-five, still dressed in hospital scrubs, Sharon steered her bicycle toward Police Headquarters—thinking unhappy thoughts about Andrew Ballantine. Because it had been a quiet afternoon in the E.R., she'd been able to spend hours on her cell phone, talking first to Greg Grimes, then to Daniel Hartman and then to Emma Neilson, Ann Trask and Gordie Pollack. The single topic of discussion: How could Andrew Ballantine, holder of a Ph.D. from Cambridge University, have been so dumb?

First, he let himself be led down the garden path by Rex Grainger.

Second, he decided on his own to visit Greg Grimes.

Third, he managed to say all the wrong things to Greg.

Fourth—and stupidest of all—he condemned Greg's beloved stained-glass doodads with faint praise.

Sharon wasn't sure what Andrew had wanted to accomplish

by his impromptu visit—but what he had done in fact was to start a big brouhaha within the Glory Community Church community. And now, she'd been given the unpleasant chore of putting out the fire. That would come after her equally apprehensive "dialogue" with Special Agent Keefe.

Sharon pedaled west on Campbell Street. Ahead on her right was Glory Police Headquarters, a single-story redbrick building. She coasted to a stop next to the bike rack alongside the front door, locked her bicycle to a crossbar and dropped her helmet in the cargo basket behind her seat.

The desk sergeant sitting in a kiosk inside the lobby pointed toward a distant door and said, "You'll find Ty Keefe in the conference room at the rear of the bullpen."

She walked quickly, avoiding eye contact with the police officers working at their desks, pondering if her mere presence in the building made them assume she had committed a crime.

The conference room was windowless, painted an institutional lime green. The wall opposite the doorway was paneled with shiny whiteboard squares that shimmered luminously beneath four large fluorescent fixtures set into the ceiling. Agent Keefe sat on one side of a large table, his bald head glowing eerily under the bluish lights. He stood when he saw her and gestured at a battered metal chair.

"Sorry about the heat wave." He mopped his forehead with a folded square of paper toweling. "This room has a bad thermostat and gets uncomfortably hot. That's why I have to leave the door open."

His voice sounded soft and affable—and not as threatening as she feared it might be. Nonetheless, she didn't believe the thermostat had failed. She'd read enough police-procedural novels to know that detectives crank up the heat to make interviewees sweat. An uncomfortable suspect is a talkative suspect.

At least, we'll both sweat.

He smiled and said, "Thank you for consenting to this meeting, Sharon."

"Did I have a choice?"

His response was a more menacing smile—the kind of predatory "lean and hungry look" that Shakespeare had attributed to Cassius in his play *Julius Caesar.*

"You might have said no," he said, "and I might have had you brought in for formal questioning by a Glory police officer. I prefer a cordial, nonconfrontational approach whenever possible. It leaves us both in a better mood."

"Are you going to read me my rights?"

"Ouch!" He grimaced as if she'd kicked him. "Why on earth would you see a need for a Miranda warning, Sharon? You're not in custody today. You're free to go any time you get bored." He heaved a deep sigh. "I assumed that *you of all* people would want to help catch the person who tried to poison Andrew Ballantine."

More than you know, she thought. But then, the import of what Agent Keefe said caught up to her. *You of all people.* Did he know that Andrew had kissed her last night—and that she had kissed him back? He might, if Andrew had told him, but that didn't seem right. She'd heard something sinister in Keefe's tone, an "I've got a secret" flavor that triggered a fresh burst of anxiety.

What did he mean by "you of all people"?

Sharon tried to gauge if her newfound nervousness showed on her face or in her gestures. She'd read somewhere that good detectives studied non-verbal communication and were experts at reading body language. Touching your chin meant you were thinking…touching your nose signaled you were lying.

She clasped her hands together and rested them on the table. Keefe could make of it whatever his suspicious mind…then the truth suddenly dawned on her.

"You jerk!" She stood up so she could look down at Agent Keefe. "I just figured it out. You've been following me."

"And, your point is?" The big man shrugged then grinned. "I arranged for you to be followed because I considered it essential to establish the precise relationship you have with Andrew Ballantine. It seems to be a tad friendlier than you admitted to me the other day. We have a fascinating video shot last night that proves the point."

"Our relationship *became* friendlier during the five days since I talked to you."

"One of you is an outstandingly fast worker."

"You can stuff that remark up your surveillance camera." She shook her finger at him. "And you can dig until you run out of dirt, but you won't find a previous connection between Andrew and me. We met on the Sunday he arrived in Glory. *Last* Sunday."

His smile became even more toxic. He waved her back into her chair and said, "Let's stop pussyfooting around, Nurse Pickard. I'd prefer that we cut to the chase."

"Mince no words," she said with an obvious dash of mockery. "Tell it like it is."

Keefe glared at her, plainly not amused. "The NCSBI's forensic lab confirmed what Rafe Neilson suspected, that the chocolates you gave Andrew Ballantine were chock-full of oleandrin. Each cordial contained several lethal doses—and was deadlier than a whole helping of Strathbogie Mist."

Sharon lifted her eyebrows. Keefe had remembered—and correctly pronounced—the name of the dessert she'd made. The man had done his homework.

"For accuracy's sake, I'll remind you that I *brought* the box to Andrew. It was a gift from someone else. When it was delivered to the information kiosk in the lobby, the gal on duty looked up Andrew's information and saw my name. She called me, and I volunteered to deliver the candies."

"So you claim…" He left the implied accusation hanging. "The facts we *know* are as follows. The wrapped box of chocolates was placed in Glorious Messengers' after-hours drop-off box some time before the company opened on Thursday morning. A plain white envelope taped to the wrapping paper contained delivery instructions, the delivery fee and a gratuity for the messenger." Keefe pointed his finger at Sharon. "We don't know who arranged the delivery to the hospital. You could be responsible."

"That's pure speculation…" she began, but Keefe kept talking.

"Okay, back to facts. Glory of Chocolate products are available at seventeen different locations in Glory to gift shops, boutiques, restaurants, even a gas station—and at dozens more in Elizabeth City, Hertford, and Edenton. Cordial cherries are especially popular at Christmas because kids like them better than truffles. They're a favorite purchase by aunts and grandmothers. We don't know when our candies were made, because the date stamp was on the cellophane wrapper that the poisoner removed.

"My theory," he went on, "is that poisoner bought two boxes of cherry cordials, so that he or she would have extras to practice the tricky job of injecting the oleandrin through the chocolate shell."

"That's another guess." She jutted her jaw and tried for a resolute expression. Keefe probably thought that she looked ridiculous. He slapped the table with his palm—an exceedingly resolute gesture.

"What we have here is a pair of attempted murders in one week. The second go-round was especially nasty. There was sufficient poison in that box of chocolates to kill two-dozen people. The poisoner didn't know how many people would be there when the box was opened—all of whom might have sampled the candy and died along with the intended victim."

"You mean people like me. If Emma Neilson hadn't become suspicious—if I'd had eaten one of those candies—I might be dead right now."

He smirked. "If you really intended to follow through with that particular chocolate cherry."

"What does that mean?"

"Taking a small bite of the candy would have made you slightly sick—which might have been enough to divert my suspicion. That's smart *and* slick at the same time."

"But why would a smart and slick gal like me personally deliver the poisoned chocolates to Andrew? That seems a remarkably foolish thing to do."

Keefe's black eyes suddenly brimmed with compassion and goodwill, as if he were playing bad cop, good cop all by himself. "I'm a straightforward, almost simpleminded detective," he said. "There's nothing fancy about the way I conduct an investigation. I gather as many facts as I can, and then invent hypotheses to explain them."

"And one of your fancy guesses is that I want to poison Andrew Ballantine, the man you watched me kiss last night." She hoped he caught her scorn.

Keefe cocked his head sideways. "Lots of homicides start with kisses, Sharon. Jealousy and revenge are two of the leading motives for murder."

"Have you guessed at my motive for murder yet?"

"I don't know yet. In this case, I may understand the details before the motive. Let's look at more facts, Nurse Pickard. Then we'll reason together." He plowed on, without waiting for her to agree. "Our anonymous poisoner is highly skilled—he or she knows how to prepare and administer lethal poisons. Not many civilians have those skills, so I theorize that the poisoner has a high level of chemical and medical knowledge. The kind of knowledge a nurse like yourself would readily have, or could readily acquire."

In spite of herself, Sharon nodded. *Stop going along with him. He's trying to get you to confess.*

"I've checked," he went on. "You keep six different books about poisons and poisoning in the E.R."

"Of course we do. We use them as reference materials whenever we treat poisoning victims."

"Exactly! Consequently, the required knowledge is available at your fingertips. And so is the means to fill the chocolate cherries with oleandrin solution. You have access to an unlimited supply of hypodermic syringes and needles in the E.R."

Sharon wanted to laugh at the absurdity of the Keefe's thinking. How could a smart investigator come up with such a goofy theory? He made as much sense as the incompetent copper in a classic murder mystery. She chuckled to herself. This would be the point in the story when the amateur sleuth revealed what she had discovered all by herself. *And the poisoner is the very last person you might imagine…*

Sharon thought about her own sleuthing efforts. She'd meant to gather the "symptoms of the crime," but all she'd accumulated were a few simple facts—Emma had provided the names of the people who'd attended the tea party. Andrew's Web site offered a list of his consulting clients, and a textbook on poisoning let her estimate the probable time Andrew had consumed the oleander toxin: close to five o'clock.

She'd run into the same brick wall that Agent Keefe had hit. What was the poisoner's motive? Why did he or she want Andrew dead? Until she could answer that question, her personal investigation wouldn't get far.

And then he put a cherry on the cupcake of his silly supposition. "I'm going to crank up my investigation, Nurse Pickard. You'll be seeing more of me in the days ahead."

"I look forward to our little talks," she said cheerfully, although she recoiled at the thought that she'd become a full-fledged suspect—or at least "a person of interest." It made no sense for Keefe to think that she'd poisoned Andrew, but most of what had happened to her this Christmas season was as non-sensical as Sugar Plum Fairies.

"Once again, we finished with time to spare," he said proudly.

Finished what? Sharon wondered as she unlocked her bicycle. This so-called "dialogue" had been a monologue, with Keefe doing most of the talking.

He's as confused as you are, Sharon realized. He can't answer the key question: Why does anyone want to kill Andrew. *He's using you to talk the puzzle through.*

That's as crazy as a nutcracker coming to life.

TWELVE

Andrew perched on the narrow seat and began to pedal his rented bicycle along the bike path in Founders' Park. He started out slowly, first wobbling to the left then wobbling right, as he waited for his sense of balance to conquer ten years of traveling everywhere by car.

The last time he'd ridden a bicycle was in England, when he was a student at Cambridge University. But Sharon loved bicycling and he would learn to love it just as much—even if regaining his skills killed him.

Whoever tried to poison me should have lent me a bicycle instead.

He veered from side to side and struggled to keep the bike upright. The saleswoman at Wheels of Glory had urged him to wear a helmet. He'd argued with her and won—"No one over sixteen is required by law to wear a helmet"—but wished that he hadn't.

I may see Sharon this afternoon after all—when I crash, and end up in the emergency room.

He'd spent the day thinking about her. Hadn't seen her for twenty hours—much too long an absence after a first kiss.

Tomorrow is Saturday, her day off. We'll go somewhere together. Maybe by bicycle.

Andrew pedaled a little faster and rediscovered that faster was easier. His self-assurance returned as the bike "stiffened." He sat more loosely, began to breathe easier, and relaxed his death grip on the handlebars. By the time the bike path wound back to Oliver Street, he felt sufficiently confident in his ability to tackle the ride south on Broad Street during Glory's afternoon rush hour.

He reached Glory Regional Hospital a few minutes after five and saw Sharon—in her signature red jacket—at the rack near the front door, unlocking her bicycle.

"How about some company on your ride home?" he said.

Sharon spun around and launched the astonished grin he'd anticipated. Probably the last thing she'd expected was to see him atop a bicycle. But her expression abruptly changed to a glower.

"We have to talk!" she snapped.

Her gruff manner dumbfounded him. She was obviously angry at him…but why?

"Okay," he managed to say. "Let's talk."

"Not here. Turn on your lights and follow me." She gestured eastward with her chin.

Without saying another word, she climbed on her bike and headed north on Broad Street. He watched her for several seconds, saw her turn right on Main Street, then recognized that she wasn't going home—nor planned to wait for him to catch up. He found the on switch for the dynamo that powered his bike's headlight and taillight and began to pedal furiously, doing his best to keep her in sight.

Andrew pumped the cranks as fast as he could, but Sharon had better-toned bicycling muscles and pedaled faster, adding to the distance between them. This part of Glory was mostly flat, so accelerating was relatively easy. Still, trying to match Sharon's pace made the tops of his thighs burn.

The sun had set minutes earlier, but some rays remained in the sky. The Christmas lights on Main Street glowed more brightly than the streetlamps, which had not fully warmed up. He found it difficult to spot Sharon's tiny taillight a block or two ahead. But the strips of reflective material sewn to the back of her red jacket helped him keep track of her in the bike lane next to the curb on the right side of the street.

What's gone wrong?

Where was the hug he'd hoped to receive? Or the welcoming kiss he'd longed for? He hadn't imagined the previous night. He'd kissed her and she'd kissed him back. What could have happened to change her feelings so dramatically?

Don't think! Pedal!

He saw her turn left on Front Street. Twenty seconds later she turned right on Campbell. Andrew knew enough of Glory's geography to guess that she was leading him toward Albemarle Sound. Perhaps she had a favorite destination close to the water?

He arrived at The Strand and saw that she'd hopped a curb and ridden along the grass-covered strip adjacent to the water. She stopped next to a bench that faced the Sound. She dismounted and extended the bike's kickstand. When Andrew reached her, she was sitting on the bench, staring doggedly at the water, her closed body language showing colossal displeasure. The soft wind coming ashore put a chill in the air, but the coolness emanating from Sharon was far icier.

What a waste!

He gazed at Albemarle Sound awhile and thought *This has to be one of Glory's most romantic locations.* The bench was more than thirty feet from the nearest streetlamp, which cast a gentle glow. He imagined his arm around Sharon, both of them watching the color of the water change as the evening deepened. What a perfect opportunity to talk about their future. But Sharon's grim demeanor destroyed any notions of a romantic encounter.

"Are you going to tell me what's wrong?" he said, trying to contain the exasperation in his voice. "I can see that you're royally teed-off about something, but I don't have a clue how I've made you mad."

"You really are dense," she said, her eyes still locked on the water.

He sat down next to her and reached for her fingers. She pulled her hand away and thrust it into her jacket pocket.

"I assume that you brought me out here for a reason."

She yanked her hand out of her pocket. "Do you have an explanation for...*this?*"

She dropped "this" into his hand then directed the beam of a penlight toward his lap. Andrew unfolded the square of paper and found the front page of the *Glory Gazette*. He scanned it swiftly in the dim light.

"When Rex Grainger asked to interview me, I thought that he needed help understanding the details of painted stained-glass windows. I didn't know that he planned to write a separate article about me."

"You must have had some inkling. After all, you said so *many* quotable things to Rex." She tore the clipping out of his hand, leaving a small fragment of newsprint between his thumb and index finger. She aimed her small flashlight and read a few passages aloud. The anger in her voice increased with each sentence she spoke.

"According to Dr. Andrew Ballantine, noted Cambridge-trained art historian, 'a failure to restore *The Pearl of Great Value* window using Daniel Cottier's original cartoon will do irreparable damage to the city's artistic and historic heritage. It's not much of an exaggeration to say that any church elder who votes to abandon a recognized masterpiece will commit the sin of cultural murder.'"

She took a breath and went on. "The elders of Glory Community Church have lost sight of the importance of the fabulous artwork in their care. They seem ready to replace a recognized national treasure with an alternative window designed by a mediocre artist who can create an illustration that requires no effort to understand. This shows a total indifference to the nature of art, plus an inexcusable lack of good sense on their part. They seem to have forgotten that the five painted stained-glass windows at Glory Community Church enrich the city and have become important tourist attractions."

Another breath. "Ballantine points out that, 'For more than one hundred and fifty years, the sensible members of Glory Community Church took delight in *The Pearl of Great Value* window. But now, a group of elders has arbitrarily concluded that today's parishioners don't like the parable or Cottier's visual interpretation of its message. I find the change in attitude bewildering.'"

She exhaled again. "Ballantine concluded by complaining to this editor that key church elders have all but ignored his unique expertise in the field of stained-glass church windows. 'The church brought me in as consultant, but the decision makers have inexplicably decided to go their own way. Jesus could have been talking about the elders of Glory Community when he asked *Can a blind man lead a blind man? Will they not both fall into a pit? Luke 6:39.*'"

Andrew took comfort sitting in the dark. If he kept his face in the shadows, Sharon wouldn't see the shame coloring his face. How could he have acted so naively? Talking freely with Rex Grainer had been a duffer's mistake. Andrew had a decade of experience interacting with the media. He knew that nothing said to a reporter was really "off-the-record," but he'd stupidly allowed Rex to feed his vanity and extract comments he should never have made.

Andrew winced at the thought that Rex—a small-town editor—had played him so skillfully.

Rex had begun by reminding Andrew what had happened at the special elders' meeting—how Greg Grimes had sandbagged Andrew with unexpected opposition to his sensible suggestion to restore *The Pearl of Great Value*. And then Rex reminded Andrew how the church had hired an expert, but had chosen to ignore his advice. And finally, Rex went on to frame his argument in more colorful language, using terms like "murder" and "arbitrary" and "blind leading the blind"—words and phrases that Andrew acknowledged were appropriate.

"For what it's worth," he told Sharon. "I never made the statements that Rex attributed to me. And I never agreed to a formal interview or to a feature article about my consulting work."

"Really? The words Rex quoted sound just like you. Who else in Glory talks about our artistic and historic heritage?" She tugged her bike helmet off her head and ran her fingers through her hair. Andrew read it as a gesture of frustration. And disappointment with him. "Did Rex Grainger lie?" Her skeptical tone signaled that she didn't believe his denial. "Did he put invented words in your mouth?"

"Not exactly. Rex talked to me about stained glass. We had a wide-ranging discussion that eventually turned to the situation at Glory Community Church. I agreed with Rex's interpretation of the mistakes the elders have made. I never intended that my offhand comments would end up—woven together, and out of context—on the front page."

Sharon tore up Grainger's article and let the pieces fall to the ground. He watched as the breeze carried them away, small white squares disappearing into the darkness.

"You make me think of a proverb my mother used to quote when I was kid," she said. "'The tongue of the wise commends knowledge, but the mouth of the fool gushes folly.' Proverbs 15:2."

Andrew laughed. What else could he do? *Foolish* was the perfect word to describe his behavior.

Sharon kept talking. "Check out the *Gazette* when you get back to The Scottish Captain. Rex wrote a long editorial that is even stronger than the article on the front page. He blasts the elders for not replacing *The Pearl of Great Value* with an exact copy. He follows with a love letter to you, urging the elders to take full advantage of your great wisdom and vast experience."

Andrew moaned.

"It gets even worse," she said. "Rex closed his critique by calling the elders late-breaking *barbarians*."

The word made Andrew flinch. He'd wondered why Greg Grimes had accused him of tagging opponents "barbarians." Where had he gotten that from?

And then, the answer flashed into Andrew's mind as he figured out what Rex Grainger had done. He'd called a few elders and told them that Andrew was bandying "barbarian" around. That allowed Rex to use the word in his editorial, while every church leader blamed Andrew.

He felt like screaming. He'd been Rex Grainger's patsy. The

editor had told everyone involved that he intended to write a scathing editorial, but he hadn't mentioned that key fact to Andrew. Sharon, too, must have heard about Rex's plans. That's why she'd been so curious about his discussion with Grainger.

She looked up at him, her emotions restrained. He would have given anything to see her joyful smile again and the way her eyes had sparkled when she looked at him in the hospital. Tonight, there was something extra in her expression. Anger? No, that had faded, leaving…*what?* The only label he could think of was…*regret.*

"Everyone I know is angry at you," she said. "The elders feel that you undermined their authority when you let yourself be interviewed by Rex Grainger. You were hired to help us fix a stained-glass window, not to climb on a soapbox and complain publicly about what the elders plan to do."

"I'm sorry that happened," he said quickly, "but all I was trying to do was…"

"Don't interrupt me! I'm not finished." She hesitated, perhaps to recapture the words she needed to say, then continued talking. "The members of WinReC feel that you undermined our committee when you visited Greg Grimes without our permission. You work for us, as our resource—in the background. We report to the elders and deal with their foibles, not you."

"Point taken. It will never happen again."

"True. Because Greg would refuse to see you. He's livid that you didn't lavish praise on his stained-glass projects. He's concluded that you're a snob—with poor judgment."

"I didn't know that Greg's a glass hobbyist. I wish someone had told me. I'll make it better tomorrow. I'll apologize for my lack of enthusiasm."

"I'm still not finished." Her voice had become softer.

"Daniel Hartman, who *never* gets upset at anyone, feels that you overstepped your role, that you've become a source of conflict inside the church. You were hired to make recommendations, to help WinReC understand the challenges we face. But you went beyond that and seemed to take charge of the restoration project. People think you want to impose a specific approach on the church. Looking back, it was a mistake for you to give a presentation to the elders, but everyone wanted to hear your opinions."

"Are you finished now?"

"Unfortunately, no."

He glanced at Sharon and saw a single tear, illuminated by the nearby streetlamp, sliding down her cheek. She didn't wipe it away.

"I don't have a choice in the matter," she said. "I've been ordered by the elders to fire you." She blinked back more tears. "The church has decided to terminate your contract as WinReC's consultant."

Andrew felt his body react in a dozen different ways. An icy pall of humiliation stabbed his innards. His shoulders slumped. His face burned. His mouth felt dry. His mind refused to accept the words Sharon had spoken.

"You can't mean that." He realized immediately how trite his response must sound to Sharon. He added, "The church needs me to help find the right parable, the right illustration and the right artist."

She had stopped looking at him and was peering at the grass near her feet. "The elders feel that you've become a stumbling block. They want WinReC to begin again—with a new consultant."

"You've told me what everyone else thinks. What about you?"

She sighed softly. And then nodded. "I agree with the elders' decision."

The damp wind felt colder. He shivered and raised his collar.

"Then you must want me to leave Glory," he said. "As quickly as I can."

"That would be best—for the church."

"And also best for you and me."

His words seemed to hang in the air, melancholy flecks blown to and fro by the breeze from the Albemarle.

She rose to her feet and, without looking at him, turned away and climbed on her bicycle.

He wanted to stop her, but what was the point? How could he stay another day in Glory? How could their relationship survive the way she felt about him?

She soon pedaled out of sight although he continued to hear the mellow clatter of her bicycle chain in the distance. The sudden ache in his heart hurt worse than the pain caused by oleandrin.

THIRTEEN

Sharon woke up with a plan for Saturday. Rather than dwell on Andrew Ballantine, she'd lock the door, curl up in her old reclining chair and spend the day watching old movies and eating chocolate. But first she needed to stock up on provisions.

At nine that morning, she bicycled across town to the Glory of Chocolate and asked for a half-pound of candy—anything *except* cherry cordials. "Make it a full pound," she corrected. She no longer cared how many zits embellished her nose. "No, I won't need it gift wrapped."

Then she visited the DVD rental shop and chose three of the longest movies on her list of favorites.

That fills eleven hours of potential moping-around time.

Finally, she stopped at Snacks of Glory and ordered a deluxe triple SOGgy Burger to go, in an insulated container.

So much for lunch...and supper.

The first twinge of regret about Andrew hit her as she bicycled east on Oliver Street. She simply didn't feel ready to go back home yet, not with thoughts of *what might have been* lurking in her consciousness. Almost without meaning to, she turned right on The Strand. She pedaled hard, enjoying the expanse of water, the brisk December air, and the dove gray sky.

Empty, cold and bleak—a perfect description of the way I feel.

"If Andrew had really cared for me, he would have stopped
me from leaving last night. He must have seen how forlorn I
was. But he didn't seem to notice my miserable mood when I
climbed on my bicycle." The wind whooshing past her head as
she whizzed west on Main Street and south on Broad Street
erased her words as soon as she spoke them. "Big surprise! Of
course Andrew doesn't care about me anymore. He thinks that
I betrayed him, that I made an irrevocable choice—I put the
church first and him second."

She felt more like laughing than crying at the situation.
Andrew might be less disappointed with her if he knew how
vigorously she had fought for him. She'd decided not to tell
him, because in the end, her impassioned defense had made no
difference. Greg Grimes had swayed the other elders against
Andrew and nothing she'd said could undo the damage. Even
Daniel Hartman believed that Glory Community Church would
be better off if Andrew returned to Asheville. And firing Andrew
was her responsibility.

*We were through the moment I told him the elders terminated
his contract.*

Almost unexpectedly, she saw The Scottish Captain ahead
on the right. Without thinking, she'd biked to the very last place
in Glory she wanted to be at this moment. She accelerated, but
then began to coast as her curiosity got the best of her. Was
Andrew's SUV still in the parking lot, or had he left Glory
without saying goodbye to her?

She steered into the lot and made a quick loop around the
perimeter. No SUV. Andrew was gone forever. The renewed
awareness saddened her immensely. She'd be alone this Christmas after all, and she had no one to blame but herself. She

couldn't point fingers at faithless husbands or even a bad matrimonial luck. She'd done what had to be done—and she'd paid the price.

The Captain's back door opened and Emma Neilson called, "Come inside, I brewed a fresh pot of coffee."

Sharon wasn't in a visiting mood, but Emma would be hurt if she rode away without an explanation. She leaned her bike against the bird feeder post opposite the kitchen window.

"You're in luck." Emma gave her a huge hug. "Calvin cooked a fabulous frittata this morning. There's a piece left with your name on it."

"I'm not hungry."

"That won't make any difference—not with Calvin's Deluxe Christmas Frittata."

Sharon followed Emma into the kitchen and tried to identify the different smells. Sautéed onions of course, hot olive oil, garlic, fried potatoes and *something else.* She sniffed once or twice and finally recognized the smell of sage, chestnuts and turkey. Calvin had incorporated a traditional Christmas dinner into a breakfast omelet.

Emma hugged her again and said, "I can see you spent part of the night crying…and I know the reason why. So you don't have to say anything. The word gets around quickly in Glory."

"Ah. I suppose that Andrew told you we've broken up."

"*What!* I didn't even know that you were a twosome." She paused while the grandfather clock in the corridor chimed ten o'clock. "Daniel called this morning with the news that you sacked Andrew. That's all I've heard."

Sharon saw no point to providing a detailed explanation. She began with a shrug. "Andrew and I had one of the shortest romances on record. Did he leave this morning?"

"Not in the way you mean. He didn't show up for breakfast today, but he hasn't checked out of his room. His belongings are still upstairs. I have no idea where he is or when he'll be back."

Sharon took a bite of frittata. *Fabulous as promised.* It didn't make any difference where Andrew had gone today. All that mattered was he'd soon leave Glory. He had no reason to say. She'd seen to that.

"I don't suppose you'd like any advice from me," Emma asked.

"That depends. You aren't going to be like Job's friends and remind me this is all my fault, are you? I know that already."

Emma laughed. "Actually, I was going to say that your happiness is more important than a church window, no matter how historic it is. If you've really fallen for Andrew, quit the WinReC, tell Greg Grimes to get a life and stand by your man. You've done more than enough for Glory Community Church this year."

"Where were you yesterday? The problem is I didn't stand by my man. I let Andrew down—I truly hurt him. I saw the pain I caused in his eyes. He'll never forgive me, no matter what I do." She laid her fork across her plate. Not even Calvin Constable's blissful frittata could get past the lump of ice that abruptly formed in her stomach when she saw that Andrew's SUV was missing. "Besides, I don't want to quit. I'm determined to see the window restoration project to the end. I won't leave Daniel in the lurch."

"And I won't stop bugging you to reconsider. You *are* in love with Andrew. I can hear it in the way you talk about him— which certainly proves to *me* that you can't be responsible for poisoning him."

Sharon understood immediately. Rafe must have told Emma that Agent Keefe considered Sharon his prime suspect.

"Thanks for caring." She stood up and kissed Emma's cheek. "I'd better go— I have a lot of nothing to do today."

"Will we see you at church tomorrow?"

"That may depend on how many zits I see on my nose tomorrow morning."

"What?"

"Don't mind me, I'm babbling gibberish."

Sharon awoke the next morning when something tugged on her fingers, which no longer seemed fully connected to her body. She opened her eyes and realized that she'd spent the night in her recliner, sitting on the TV remote control, leaning against her right arm. Heather, her Scottish terrier, was nibbling her hand— an appendage that currently felt as numb as a piece of wood.

She stretched and rubbed her arm to restore the circulation. Heather immediately turned her attention to the box of chocolate on the side table. The white Scottie sniffed the edge of the table, looking for an opportunity to pounce.

"No chocolate for pooches, Lassie," Sharon said. "We've had enough poisonings this week in Glory."

Heather glared unhappily at Sharon, then began to bark, soft little yaps that signaled she wanted to go outside. Sharon stepped into her slippers and Heather, excited by the response, began to run circles around her.

Sharon unlocked her back door and led Heather into her enclosed back garden. "Please hurry up—I'm not wearing a coat over my sweatsuit and it's freezing out here."

Heather trotted around the garden, leaving indented paw prints on the frosty grass, apparently enjoying the cold. After visiting a convenient patch of grass, she picked up a rubber toy and bounded past Sharon, her tail wagging.

"Sorry, young lady, but I'm not in the mood to play this morning. I'm still too depressed. It was a mistake to watch these tearjerkers—they all made me think about Andrew. I should have rented a trio of horror films."

Heather seemed to understand. She pushed open the ajar back door and trotted over to her food bowl in the corner of the kitchen. As Sharon filled the bowl, she found herself thinking about MacTavish, Andrew's Scottie. Was Andrew back in Asheville this morning feeding him? Curiously, everything she saw or did yesterday invoked memories of Andrew. The old movies. The glory of chocolate candies she ate. The SOGgy Burger. Her bike ride along The Strand. Eating at The Scottish Captain. The Christmas decorations all over Glory.

Had she really pushed Andrew out of her life for good? The question surfaced every time she thought about him. There could be only one answer, but the notion that she'd never see him again was almost too much to bear.

She sat on her sofa and drew her knees to her chest. From across the room, Heather studied her mistress. When Sharon didn't call her name, the Scottie closed her eyes and fell asleep, her little doggie brain clearly not concerned with church windows, or male pride or fruitless arguments about what an obscure parable really means.

Get over it! You have to learn to live without Andrew Ballantine.

Her telephone rang. Could it be Andrew? She lunged for the receiver.

"Good morning!" Emma positively bubbled. "It's your friendly neighborhood innkeeper and chauffeur. Rafe and I decided that the thing we want to do most this morning is pick you up and drive you to church."

"I live one long block from Glory Community Church."

"Nonetheless, we refuse to take no for an answer. Be ready at ten-thirty."

"Well…"

"The only thing you can say is yes. We're not going to let you miss the last Advent worship service before Christmas."

"Thank you, Mommy." Sharon made her voice drip with sarcasm.

But later, as she sat in a crowded pew, with Gordie Pollack on her left and Ann Miller Trask on her right, Sharon said a silent "thanks be to God" that her best friend had gone the extra mile this morning. She waved at Emma and Rafe, both in the choir, and looked forward to the time when she would be singing again.

The sanctuary was full today, with many "seasonal" worshipers and an equal number of visitors she'd never seen before. Amanda Turner was sitting three pews back. She fluttered her fingers at Sharon and offered an animated smile. Sharon waved back. Perhaps her first impressions of Amanda had been wrong? Maybe they could become friends—now that Andrew was out of the picture.

And then, out of the corner of her eye, Sharon saw Andrew in the back of the sanctuary. She spun around in her seat, oblivious to her earlier concerns. All that mattered was that he was only a few feet away, close enough for her to race to his side.

But when she looked again, he was gone. Sharon wasn't sure who she'd actually seen standing near the door. She concluded that a dose of wishful thinking had encouraged her to imagine Andrew standing close by. She stared at her knees and hoped that no one around her would notice that she was crying.

Sharon responded woodenly during the opening prayers,

hymns and praise songs. She hadn't read the bulletin, so when Daniel began his sermon, the topic startled her. Daniel's message was about understanding parables.

"Good morning, my friends. I'd like you to crank your imaginations into high gear. Try to imagine me as a rabbi in the first century. Yes I'd have a beard, and yes my hair would be significantly longer, and yes I probably be wearing an elaborate hat.

"Now imagine that someone says, 'Rabbi, can you tell me more about the Kingdom of Heaven—the time of God's reign promised in the Hebrew Scriptures?'

"Well, Rabbi Daniel might reply, 'The Kingdom of Heaven is like treasure hidden in a field. When a man found it, he hid it again, and then in his joy went and sold all he had and bought that field.'

"I can hear you thinking, Wait a minute! That sounds very much like one of Jesus' parables—the parable of *The Hidden Treasure,* recorded in Matthew 13:44.

"You'd be right. Historians tell us that the rabbis of Jesus' time commonly used parables to teach moral and life principles. It's quite possible that Rabbi Jesus retold a popular parable of the day.

"The Kingdom of Heaven is like hidden treasure… I can't help but wonder if the faithful who heard that particular parable two millennia ago understood what it meant. The answer seems to be that first-century worshipers had several different interpretations. That's one of the interesting things about many familiar parables—they can have multiple *true* meanings, not just one."

Daniel's gaze met hers and he smiled, almost as if he were talking just to her…? She sat higher in her pew as Daniel went on.

"For example…it's perfectly sensible to conclude that the

Kingdom of Heaven has great value—ultimately more than everything else a person might own. But that's only one possible interpretation.

"It's equally true to point out that some people may 'walk past' the Kingdom of Heaven without ever finding it.

"And it's also correct to decide that each of us has a personal responsibility to acquire the treasure of the Kingdom of Heaven—to make it our own."

"Three different interpretations, all of them valid." Daniel held up three fingers. "We can't insist that one is more correct than the others, because this is one of the parables that Jesus didn't explain.

"We learn something important from the notion that specific teachings in the Bible have different interpretations. It means that it's okay for Christians to see some things differently. We all agree on the basics, that Jesus, the Son of God, died to put us right with God. But we can have different opinions about what the parables are trying to tell us…or what's the most appropriate illustration when we rebuild the damaged window in this sanctuary. Diversity of this kind can be useful, because it expands our horizons and gives us different perspectives on the Kingdom of Heaven—and other important Christian teachings.

"Our elders will soon choose a course of action for our window. Some of you will agree with their decision, some of you won't. But we can't allow a stained-glass window to cause a rift at Glory Community Church—certainly not at Christmas, the time of the year when Christians traditionally come together.

"Whatever your opinions about *The Pearl of Great Value,* remember that we are united in Christ."

Sharon heard several people around her say "Amen," but she merely nodded. Her mind was locked on Andrew. Where was he? What could she do to mend their rift?

She jumped to her feet after Daniel spoke the benediction. She squeezed past the other worshipers, determined to race home. Emma reached her first.

"Nice try!" Emma said. "But futile! Rafe's outside, guarding the doors. Abandon all thoughts of escaping. You're having lunch with us today."

"You'll rue your invitation. I'm in a stinky mood."

"That's what friends are for."

Sharon let Emma lead her through the narthex. There were dozens of men making for the exit, none of them as tall as Andrew. A spark of optimism ignited inside her heart. Perhaps she had seen him earlier?

She felt herself smile for the first time since Friday night.

FOURTEEN

Andrew spent Saturday on North Carolina's Outer Banks, walking on sand dunes near the Currituck Beach Lighthouse, watching shore birds, and mulling over how he'd botched everything he'd attempted in Glory. He'd failed miserably trying to save an artistic masterpiece. He'd crashed and burned supporting the WinReC. And he'd made a complete mess of *wooing* Sharon Pickard—to use a vintage word still popular in Scotland.

Being fired didn't bother him. Every consultant knew that some assignments didn't work out, mostly because of mismatches in people chemistry. Far more painful to deal with was his conviction that he'd disappointed Sharon—that he'd let her down.

What could he have done differently? Number one on the list: He should have refused to speak to Rex Grainger. Agreeing to an open-ended interview had been foolish. He should have known from the get-go that Rex disagreed with the elders, that he intended to use the pages of the *Glory Gazette* to advocate his position, and that he saw Andrew as a bludgeon to drive home his argument.

Andrew might have also done more research on Glory Community Church. Perhaps he could have learned in advance how the church leaders felt about *The Pearl of Great Value* window?

Lastly, he might have gone home after he was poisoned. That

had been a rather strong omen of unpleasant things to come. He hadn't wanted to believe that he'd been attacked on purpose, but the second attempt left little room for doubt. Someone had tried to kill him—even though he couldn't name a single personal or professional enemy. The only possibility, outlandish as it seemed, was that somebody at Glory Community Church hated the old window enough to want him dead.

Andrew made two decisions when he awoke on Sunday morning: First he would attend church. Second, the church would be Glory Community. Once he felt right with God, he'd pack his bags, tidy up the loose ends of his consulting assignment and prepare to leave Glory at first light on Monday.

His most challenging responsibility still unfulfilled was to write a final report that summarized his recommendations. He owed the church his best judgment, even though the elders would probably shred the report before anyone read it.

They think I'm a jerk—and it's mostly my fault that they do.

"I'm glad to see you today!" The owner of the voice sounded as if he really meant his words.

Andrew looked over his shoulder into Daniel Hartman's convivial grin. Andrew was standing next to his SUV, which he'd parked in the northwest corner of Glory Community Church's parking lot. He'd been using the open door to shield him from worshippers walking past.

Daniel pointed to a brick house just beyond the shrubbery that edged the parking lot. "That's the church's manse. That's where I live."

When Andrew nodded Daniel went on, "Why did you park so far from the side entrance?"

"I feel a tad awkward running into people I know this morning. I'm sure you'll understand why."

"I am duty bound to remind you that you never have to feel awkward around God."

"True! But God's not an elder or a member of the WinReC."

Daniel laughed. "Catch me after the service. I'd love to hear your opinion on my message today."

Andrew waited in the parking lot until most of the worshipers had disappeared inside the church. Then he made his way into the rear of the sanctuary. He spotted Gordie and Sharon immediately, sitting a dozen pews closer to the front. Andrew leapt into the narthex when he saw Sharon start to turn her head. Chances were good she hadn't caught sight of him. Splendid! He didn't have the courage to face her. Not yet.

Andrew had listened to the service with his ear pressed against the door that led from the narthex as to the sanctuary. He thought Daniel's message about interpreting parables intriguing. Perhaps some of the elders who thought *The Pearl of Great Value* bewildering would give the parable a second chance?

Probably not. They rejected the parable more enthusiastically than they rejected you.

Andrew decided to leave before the congregation finished singing the responsive hymn. The fewer people that saw him, the better.

He literally bumped into Amanda Turner as they both stepped through the front door at the same time. She let out a large guffaw. "I always say never get in front of a man who's trying to leave church."

He offered a quick apology.

"No need, darlin'. In fact, you've made my day less lonely." She followed him down the church's front steps. "By the way, can I count on you comin' to my Christmas Eve shindig?"

Rats! A loose end you overlooked.

"I won't be able to attend, Amanda, because I'm leaving Glory tomorrow morning."

"Oh! Pooh! There'll be no one worth talkin' to if you're not there. And when you say leavin' Glory, you can't possibly mean for good."

"My consulting assignment is over. It's time to go home."

"Then you owe me a king-size goodbye hug." She threw her arms around him. He managed not to scream as he unwound from her brawny embrace. He jogged to his SUV and didn't look back.

Andrew made a quick stop at a fast-food restaurant for a sub and a soft drink, and then drove to the Glory National Bank building. By twelve-thirty, he was in his temporary office at the Scottish Heritage Society, shoveling some miscellaneous paperwork into his attaché case and the rest into a wastebasket.

He'd almost finished tidying his desk when he noticed a thick manila envelope that had his name scrawled in large letters on the front. He undid the clasp and slid out a sheaf of drawings—perhaps twenty in all—obviously the work of children.

You forgot about the contest you agreed to judge.

Andrew browsed through the entries quickly. Most of the drawings echoed the visual themes in Daniel Cottier's original window. Lots of pearl-colored "baseballs." Lots of household goods and jewelry up for auction. Lots of merchants toting bags of money.

Most of the entries, but not all. Andrew found one drawing that was impossible to decipher. A kid named Brandon DeWitt had done a messy marker rendering that showed the merchant bouncing up and down, his legs thrashing, his feet not touching the ground. Andrew had no idea what the drawing meant—and he doubted that Brandon did either. The weird illustration was probably his way of protesting the requirement that he create an entry for the contest.

Why did the name Brandon ring a bell? Andrew abruptly re-membered. He must be the grandson of Aaron DeWitt, the "elderly elder" with thick gray hair who couldn't explain the parable's meaning. No wonder the kid's illustration was so confused.

"Ladies and gentlemen, we have our winner." Andrew laughed as he held up Brandon's "artwork." Let his grandfather and the elders figure out what the kid was trying to communi-cate. They were the self-declared experts at interpreting parables.

Andrew wrote "Winner" on a yellow sticky and affixed it near the top of Brandon's drawing. He returned the stack of entries to the manila envelope, placed it in Gordie's "In" basket, and resumed tidying up.

He heard a key turn in the front-door lock, followed by a burst of Gordie Pollack's inimitable, trill-filled Scottish brogue: "Dr. Ballantine, I presume."

"You presume correctly, if too much."

Gordie poked his head around the door frame. "I saw you in church today. I figured you might come here to pick up your things." He stepped into the conference room that was Andrew's temporary office. "I'm pretty sure that Sharon also saw you. You should have come over. It's obvious that she misses you."

"Another meeting might be difficult for both of us."

Gordie held up a paper bag. "Coffee? I decided it was easier to buy than make for only two."

"I'd love a cup."

"Who else have you talked to since Friday night?" Gordie asked. "I mean among elders or WinReC members?"

"No one. I said hello to Daniel this morning."

"Did he tell you about our conference call on Friday afternoon?"

Andrew shook his head.

"I thought not," Gordie said. "Consequently, you don't realize that you owe Sharon a whopping thank-you. As well as a big kiss." He smiled. "The word is out that you two were an item."

Andrew shrugged. "We were, until she fired me."

"She had to do that. What you don't know is that she fought like a mother grizzly bear to keep you as our consultant. She said that the church hired you for your unique expertise—a hard-won commodity you acquired *because* of your passion for stained-glass windows. She reminded the elders that you didn't do anything other than fight for what you thought was right, that your integrity prevented your from doing anything else."

"She said that?"

"At least twice. The battle went back and forth for nearly a half-hour. I thought that Sharon was going to win, until Greg Grimes finally locked the other elders in his camp by reading the silly statements you made to the *Glory Gazette.*" Gordie peeled back the plastic lid on his coffee cup. "I wouldn't be surprised if she tries to defend you again on Monday night."

"What happens tomorrow night?"

"The Elders Board's formal December meeting. The WinReC is now on the agenda. A last-minute addition."

"I get it. The elders have to make my firing official."

Gordie nodded. "Sorry about that."

Andrew hid his befuddled reaction as best he could. He'd misjudged Sharon. She understood his motives after all—and had defended him publicly. But her actions raised more questions than they answered. Why had she left him sitting in the dark? Why did she bicycle away before he had a chance to change her mind? It had been clear to him as the lights on the Albemarle's shoreline that she didn't want to be stopped—that she didn't even want him to try.

"Can I give you some advice?" Gordie asked.

"Why not? Dozens of other people in Glory have."

"Call Sharon. Better yet, go to see her."

"I'll think about it."

"Don't think too long, my friend. Sharon Pickard is a keeper." Gordie extended his hand. "In the event I don't see you again before you leave Glory—*well*, you know, *cheerio, cheery-bye* and *lang may yer lum reek!*"

Andrew stood up. "Thanks, Gordie. May you live long and stay well, too. Godspeed. And thanks for explaining how Sharon supported me."

When Gordie left, Andrew pondered his advice. It seemed simple enough—run to her side. But then what? They had fought about his work; the inevitable problem had ruined another relationship. Would he ever be able to tell her that she was more important than his work? The words were easy to say—but would he ever really mean them?

Think about Sharon later. You have a report to write.

Andrew began to plan the report the for elders that would summarize his final recommendations. He decided that the best starting point would be the two-fold "compromise" he'd offered Sharon. On the one hand, he would suggest a less-confusing alternative parable for the new window. On the other hand, he would recommend an appropriate stained-glass artist to execute the new cartoon.

Proposing a suitable artist would be easy. He had a long list of good candidates in his address book. That would give Sharon's committee a head start toward creating a credible replacement window. After that, they'd be on their own, although Sharon had met Franny Brewer and could rely on her window-crafting skills.

Identifying an alternative parable was more problematic. How could he recommend a substitute when no one had the vaguest idea why *The Pearl of Great Value* had been included among the five parables chosen one hundred fifty years ago? Who had made the original decision? Daniel Cottier? James Ballantine? The nineteenth-century leaders of Glory Community Church? The anonymous church architect who had designed the sanctuary?

Andrew had asked repeatedly, but neither the church's records nor the Ballantine family archives had provided an answer.

Could the five parables Cottier illustrated have been grouped together by accident? Andrew didn't think so, even though the stories didn't share a common theological theme—at least not one that he could make out.

The Prodigal Son, The Lost Coin, and *The Lost Sheep* all seemed to exemplify the idea of God redeeming "lost" sinners. By contrast, *The Wise and Foolish Builders* advised Christians to build their faith atop a solid foundation, and *The Pearl of Great Value* meant…something else.

Although they taught different lessons, someone had decided a century and a half ago that the parables supported each other's message. All he had to do was find this "missing link." That would give him the key to choosing a substitute parable.

The color photograph of the destroyed window was still hanging on the conference room wall, surrounded by its four surviving colleagues. He peered at it and once again pondered the parable's meaning. Why did Jesus say that the Kingdom of Heaven is like finding a valuable pearl?

Daniel Hartman's sermon this morning hadn't resolved the confusion. If anything, Daniel had added to the chaos by giving church members permission to adopt different interpretations. But which interpretation had Daniel Cottier tried to memorialize in a stained-glass window?

Andrew fired up his laptop computer, accessed his Bible software, and reread two commentaries on Matthew 13:45-46. Neither provided much enlightenment. The authors had merely rounded up the usual suspects—popular interpretations that Andrew had seen many times before:

Things of great value are often hidden—we may have to search for them.

Before we can take hold of a truly precious find—the Kingdom of Heaven—we need to get rid of the earthly stuff we presently over-value.

When you identify something of great value, you should act quickly and decisively to acquire it.

These struck Andrew as useful teachings, but none of them seemed a concept worth communicating in a full-size stained-glass window. He moved closer to the collection of photographs and touched each of them in turn. Whoever decided to include *The Pearl of Great Value* in the five-window array must have seen something more in the story—an overarching notion that would tie the quintet of windows together.

The jolt of recognition shoved Andrew back into his chair.

He stared at the photographs from a distance and immediately saw the common theme that linked four out of the five windows. The theme that Daniel Cottier had mysteriously left out of his cartoon for *The Pearl of Great Value.*

The theme that Brandon DeWitt tried to capture in his contest entry.

Andrew raced back to Gordie's office, tore open the envelope he'd left in Gordie's inbox, and retrieved Brandon's drawing. There it was! Clear as…well, as clear as a nine-year-old could draw it.

Little Brandon had succeeded where every adult in Glory Community Church had failed. He'd identified the missing ingredient. He'd come up with a spectacular interpretation of *The Pearl of Great Value* that explained why the five parables belonged side-by-side.

Andrew had an idea.

He carefully smoothed Brandon's drawing on his desktop to remove several creases. Then he searched for the Glory telephone book. First thing on Monday morning, he would have the drawing photographed, enlarged and mounted on a large piece of foam core board.

And then, on Monday-night, I'll crash the Elder Board meeting.

He glanced at his distorted reflection in the laptop screen and saw he was smiling. No surprise there. At long last he had something useful to say about Glory Community's stained-glass windows. The elders had fired him; nothing could change that. But he would leave on a high note, making a real contribution to the restoration effort.

Now, if only you can figure out what to do about Sharon Pickard.

FIFTEEN

Emma pulled Sharon aside outside the Elder Board meeting room and said, "Andrew still hasn't checked out of The Scottish Captain."

Sharon peered at her friend. "I wonder why. What's keeping him in Glory?"

"Let me guess." Emma punctuated her words with a sly simper.

"If that were true," Sharon said, "Andrew would have called me by now. He hasn't." She let herself sigh. "We're history."

Emma made a face. "Give him time. When it comes to talking to women, most men are less bold than we think they are." She frowned more deeply. "Speaking of time, Christmas week is a busy period for innkeepers. I hope the elders don't plan to keep us long tonight. I have other, more pressing things on my plate."

Sharon bit back a smile. Emma had looked intently at her when she spoke the words "keep us long tonight." Her friend was obviously concerned that Sharon might renew the debate about firing Andrew and start a two-hour long dialogue about him.

That won't happen. More fighting would be useless. Andrew's gone for good.

"The question of Andrew Ballantine's contract was tacked

to the front of elder's agenda at the last minute," Sharon said. "Daniel knows that the members of WinReC are all suffering from meeting burnout. He promised me that we'll be out of here in ten minutes—at most."

"Praise God."

"Indeed!" Sharon added a crisp nod, although she felt a slight pang of regret. A long, boring elders meeting would give her something to do this evening. With Andrew out of her life, she might as well fill the empty hours with church business. Old movies hadn't worked for her.

Sharon took a chair along the rear wall of the room. She saw no reason to claim one of the empty seats at the conference table.

Daniel began the meeting precisely at seven, spoke a blessing, then said, "This is the December meeting of the Board of Elders. I see that we have a quorum. The first item on tonight's intentionally short agenda is a piece of new business that concerns the work of our Windows Restoration Committee." He broadcast a smile around the room. "I encourage short discussions this evening. Many of us have not finished wrapping gifts or, in my case, trimming the Christmas tree."

When no one objected, Daniel continued. "The members of Window Restoration Committee have been invited to participate in this segment of our meeting. Are they here?"

Sharon raised her hand. Gordie said, "Aye!" Ann said, "Present!" Emma waved at Daniel.

Daniel pressed on. "Elder Grimes has requested to make a motion. Greg, you have the floor."

Greg stood up. "I need to make a comment first. The elders want to apologize for 'short circuiting' the WinReC's authority in the matter of the consultant the committee selected. We know that the committee, has worked long and hard to choose the best approach for restoring our window." Greg looked at Sharon expectantly.

She rose to her feet and said, "We appreciate the elders' concern for our feelings. But the four members of the WinReC understand that specific circumstances required the elders to intervene and ultimately make the decision they did."

Greg pivoted his head back and forth, taking in all the elders. "That being said, I move that we terminate, effective immediately, the consulting agreement between the church and Dr. Andrew Ballantine, a stained-glass window consultant based in Asheville, North Carolina."

"I second the motion," said a voice from the far end of the table. Sharon didn't know, or care, who it belonged to.

Daniel spoke. "A motion has been made and seconded. Is there any discussion?"

Greg cleared his throat. "I believe that the Chair of WinReC has already notified Dr. Ballantine of church's intention to terminate his contract for a variety of reasons I will not get into right now. Let's say simply that we take different approaches to restoring the window and have different priorities."

"That's putting *much* too kind a spin on things." Andrew stepped into the room. "The elders and I haven't been able to agree on anything. We fought like cats and dogs most of last week."

Sharon heard Emma, seated across the room, groan. Emma glanced at her watch and then at Sharon, a "now we're trapped for hours" expression spreading across her face.

Sharon worked to get a grip on her own emotions. Her heart throbbed inside her chest and there was something odd about her breathing. Andrew smiled at her and made things worse. He looked incredibly handsome this evening, perhaps because he appeared more confident than he'd ever seemed before.

Sharon studied Andrew a moment and pondered what he hoped to accomplish with his dramatic entrance. And what was inside the large flat package he carried?

"Mr. Moderator…" Andrew spoke to Daniel Hartman. "I ask your indulgence. I accept that my relationship with Glory Community Church has been terminated. But I have a brief statement to make about the replacement window that I believe the elders will find both interesting and informative."

"This is highly irregular," Greg said.

"Perhaps it is," Daniel said. "But we hired Andrew to help us. Now that his assignment is over, I think he deserves an opportunity to speak. We certainly have time to hear a brief statement."

"I guess." Greg managed a shallow nod, but Sharon could feel his annoyance from ten feet away. The skin on the back of his chubby neck had become as red as his hair. He had developed an intense dislike of Andrew—more than any other elder.

Andrew approached the conference table. "I know that everyone here has read the article about me in Friday's *Glory Gazette*. Although I didn't speak the exact words that Rex Grainger 'quoted,' he masterfully summed up my attitude and opinions." Andrew offered a mischievous smile. "Looking back, if I were you, I would have fired me—even sooner."

The elders laughed, including Greg.

Andrew went on. "I have with me a final report that I wrote yesterday. I captured the situation as I see it now—which is completely different from my views of last week. The report will be the final deliverable of my short consulting assignment. Let me summarize what I've concluded."

Sharon snickered to herself. She knew he intended his dramatic pause to make his audience curious. Andrew was enjoying himself immensely, using all his rhetorical skills in his farewell performance.

"Up until yesterday afternoon," he said, "I considered *The Pearl of Great Value* window to be one of Daniel Cottier's masterpieces. I no longer do. I consider his design to be technically excellent. He created a high-quality window that fully exploited the artistic resources of stained glass. But, as many of you have tried to point out to me, the window had no heart. It was…*blah!*"

Andrew laid his flat parcel on the conference table and tore off the brown wrapping paper. Sharon recognized a large rectangle of mounting board, facedown to hide whatever was on the front side. Lying on top was the photograph of *The Pearl of Great Value* window.

He displayed the photo to the elders and said, "I've heard this illustration described as a man clearing out his attic so that he can buy a baseball."

Another laugh from the elders. They leaned forward in their chairs; Andrew had won their rapt attention. Sharon, too, was staring at him—she hoped her expression wouldn't seem too adoring to Emma, who kept looking across at her.

Andrew continued. "On Sunday, we heard a sermon from Pastor Hartman explaining that this parable has many possible meanings. As we all know, variety doesn't necessarily mean clarity. The many interpretations of *The Pearl of Great Value* within this church have caused great confusion. Unfortunately, your old stained-glass window did nothing to resolve the uncertainty.

"The easiest solution to the parable problem would be to find another teaching of Jesus to illustrate in the replacement window. There's only one reason I can think of to *not* do that.

Back in the middle of the nineteenth century, your forebears in this church settled on five parables that they felt belonged together. We don't know who suggested the five, but we can be certain that the church's leaders in 1858 affirmed the decision. If they hadn't, your particular windows would not have been built. James Ballantine was strict on that point. He insisted on unanimity among leaders before he accepted a commission."

Daniel poured a cup of water for Andrew. He took three quick sips.

"Were the nineteenth-century leaders wrong to choose *The Pearl of Great Value?* Until yesterday afternoon I thought they might be. I couldn't find a common thread linking the five parables. That's one of the reasons why so few parishioners praised the old window. It seemed an interloper, a weed invading a bed of flowers.

"Looking back, I fought to reproduce the 'dandelion' because I didn't want the church to discard a moderately well-known example of James Ballantine's work. I know now that reproducing a failed window makes as much sense as purposely planting crabgrass in a lawn."

Andrew raised his hand. "How many elders want to abandon *The Pearl of Great Value?*"

All the right hands around the table shot up.

"That's the way I felt, too," Andrew said. "Start from scratch—find a new parable, build a new window. But..." He paused. "Yesterday, I discovered a new visual interpretation of *The Pearl of Great Value.* A cartoon drawn by a brilliant local artist changed my mind. Perhaps you *can* keep the original parable? Perhaps you *can* honor the wishes expressed by those elders in 1858? Perhaps you can do these things and also create a stained-glass window that will be meaningful to today's wor-shipers. A window that everyone in the sanctuary will under-stand."

He moved close to the table and raised the mounting board so that the elders could see Brandon DeWitt's drawing.

"I know that picture," said Aaron DeWitt. "My grandson drew it."

"Okay," another elder said to Aaron. "Then maybe you can tell us what it means."

Aaron shrugged. "Don't ask me. I'm not a fan of modern art."

Andrew grinned. "I have an interpretation. I believe I'm right, although it took me quite a while to figure out Brandon's intentions. The best way to explain this drawing is with a demonstration."

Andrew handed the oversize illustration to Daniel Hartman and took several steps away from the table. He twirled around once and began to yell, "Yay! Look at me!" And then he started to jump up and down, trying to flap his feet back and forth like a ballet dancer.

Sharon wished she could vanish into her chair. *What lunacy had gotten into Andrew's head?* She refused to imagine what the elders thought of this performance.

Daniel abruptly stood up. "I get it!" he said excitedly. "I think you're absolutely right—and I'm astonished that no one else noted the mistake during the past one hundred fifty years."

"Is anyone going to let me in on the secret?" Greg asked.

"The secret is *joy,*" Andrew said. "The ordinary, jumping-around, shouting-happily joy that human beings experience when something wonderful happens." He sat on the edge of the table. "That's what was missing in Daniel Cottier's original design. He left out the joy."

He held up the photo of the old window again. "This illustration is joyless, but think about the four surviving windows. Try to recall the faces of the people in the pictures. Some of you have seen them hundreds of times—

"The father of the Prodigal is thrilled that his wayward son has returned.

"The shepherd is delighted that he's found his one Lost Sheep.

"The happy woman who found her Lost Coin throws a party to celebrate—much like the angels of God rejoice in Heaven when one previously lost sinner repents.

"The Wise Builder is ecstatic that the flood didn't damage his house."

Andrew slid the photo across the table. "But look at the merchant who bought *The Pearl of Great Value*. Cottier's design gives him the bored expression of a businessman at an auction. There's certainly no joy on his face. He seems almost indifferent that he's acquired a great treasure—the priceless pearl that represents the Kingdom of Heaven."

Sharon thought about it. The concept was so simple—the deficiency so glaring. Why hadn't the WinReC zeroed-in on joy, one of the fruits of the Holy Spirit that Paul described in Galatians 5:22?

Andrew retrieved the photograph and ripped it in half. "Consign this design to the trashcan. But consider finding a *joyful* illustration based on *The Pearl of Great Value*. That's my final recommendation to Glory Community Church." He stood up. "Thank you for listening."

"So the elders were right all along," Greg said.

"Completely right," Andrew agreed.

"And you were wrong?"

"Wholly wrong."

Sharon listened to the exchange, astonished by Andrew's willingness to admit his mistakes. What had happened to him yesterday? What had driven his newfound humility? As she looked around the room, she noted that several other elders seemed uncomfortable with Andrew accepting all the blame.

Aaron DeWitt spoke first. "The elders didn't give Andrew much help," he said. "We knew that our members didn't like *The Pearl of Great Value* window—but we couldn't explain why. That's not Andrew's fault, it's ours. And every one of us agrees that the old window was an important artistic and historic artifact. We can't fault Andrew for reminding us that's true, even if he did it a bit forcefully."

Ann Miller Trask chimed in. "I'm curious! Your great-great-great-grandfather was a wizard with stained-glass church windows. How could he have let a dud slip by?"

"I can answer that one," Greg said. "James Ballantine was a superb craftsman, but he left the design to artists like Daniel Cottier." He smiled. "I do the same thing. Consider the stained-glass transom panel over my front door. It's well made—it took more than two months to build—but the illustration I chose is a bit…*goofy.* One of these days, I'll do it over again with a better cartoon. I suppose we can do the same thing, with *The Pearl of Great Value.*"

Sharon felt like hugging Greg. He had bought into the exact compromise she wanted. Now the church could find a world-class artist—and commission a great window.

Aaron DeWitt jumped back in. "I like Dr. Ballantine's idea. We'd have five joyous windows—including one based on *The Pearl of Great Value.* That should satisfy the artists, the historians, and the people who consider our windows tourist attractions. It might even keep Rex Grainger happy—although that may be too much to hope for." Sharon watched Aaron's shoulders hunch as he turned toward Andrew. "I trust you're not suggesting that we use my grandson's drawing as the cartoon for our new window. I love Brandon, but he's not exactly…"

"Daniel Cottier." Andrew finished the elderly elder's sentence. "No. Your challenge is to find a stained-glass artist who can create a cartoon that understands the importance of joy in the parable of *The Pearl of Great Value*. An artist who can create a cartoon that will match Daniel Cottier other designs."

"That's would be quite a challenge for us," Greg said, "especially since we don't know diddly about stained-glass designers who do church windows." He cleared his throat again. "How would you go about such a project, assuming that you were still on the case?"

Sharon held her breath, not fully believing what she'd heard Gregory Grimes just say.

"I'd hold an open competition," Andrew said, "to find the right artist." He propped up Brandon's drawing again. "A more grown-up version of the contest that produced this masterpiece."

Daniel stood up. "May I remind everyone that we're discussing a motion that's been made and seconded? Does anyone want to call for a vote?"

Everyone in the room stared at Greg Grimes, who knew that all eyes were on him and all ears were waiting for him to answer the obvious question: Do you still want to fire Andrew Ballantine?

Someone at the far end of the table saved Greg. "I move that the meeting proceed to the next order of business."

Greg bounced a foot high when he shouted, "Second!"

Several elders laughed when the new motion carried unanimously. Sharon found herself laughing, too. She knew enough about the Rules of Order to understand that shifting to next item on the agenda meant that the motion to fire Andrew had been "tabled" indefinitely.

What better time for Greg to have a change of heart than Christmastime?

Sharon's musing about the season was interrupted by the abrupt realization that four of the people who'd stared at Greg Grimes were now staring at her: Emma, Gordie, Ann and Daniel. She also knew the obvious question they wanted to ask her: What happens now between you and Andrew?

"Who's going to save me?" she murmured, without thinking.

"Me, I hope."

Andrew was standing next to her. She wanted to throw her arms around him. Instead, she let him take her hand and lead her out of the room.

SIXTEEN

It seemed a moment of pure insanity.

Andrew held tight to Sharon's hand as they left the meeting room, but he had no idea where he was taking her.

What happens now?

She seemed to read his jumbled thoughts. "Let's find a quiet place where we can talk."

Talk! Yes! You need to talk to Sharon. But what are you going to say?

He'd spent hours that afternoon searching for the perfect words, but they wouldn't coalesce in his mind. He knew that he had to tell Sharon how much he felt about her, but he had no idea how to begin.

What if she won't listen? What if I make her angry again?

He'd been able to focus on parables and stained-glass windows to prepare for the meeting, but now that he was alone with Sharon, his mind went blank again. It should be simple to explain himself to her—but the prospect filled him with misgivings. One careless word, and he might lose her forever.

Judging from the smiling faces they passed, Sharon's friends seemed pleased to see her walking next to him. But how did she feel? He glanced at her, hoping to read her mood. He failed totally.

She looks so beautiful tonight.

His world seemed to tilt. He suddenly yearned to take her in his arms and kiss her. He grasped her fingers more tightly and managed to stammer, "Where…where are we going."

"To the sanctuary," she said. "No one will be there at this hour of the night."

Andrew moved closer to Sharon to signal his approval and discovered they were walking together in flawless synchronism. Their footfalls were in perfect step, so why not their heartbeats?

Don't hope for what may not be true.

He heard a door close in the distance, then laughter. The elders must be taking a break before they resumed their agenda. When they reached the sanctuary, Sharon switched on the overhead lights, illuminating the newly added boughs of pine tied together with slender gold ribbons that decorated the balcony and the ends of the pews.

"I love the smell of Christmas in a church," she murmured, her hand still locked in his.

She didn't seem to expect a reply, so he said nothing and allowed her to lead him down to the front pew. They sat near the advent wreath, four of its candles partially guttered, the white Christ candle still pristine, waiting for Christmas day. High above were the stained-glass windows that had brought them together—and then tore them apart.

He shuddered at the thought of losing Sharon forever. There was only one way to find out if he had. He put his arm around her and pulled her close. She didn't resist. He bent his head toward hers. He kissed her, felt her return his kiss.

His fear began to dissolve and he made a silent promise. *I won't let her run from me again. Please, God. Give me the right words to say to her.*

The sanctuary door opened, and Sharon abruptly pulled away.

"Oh my!" Greg Grimes said. "I didn't know anyone was in here." His voice filled with embarrassment. "I'll come back later."

"Don't go," Andrew and Sharon said almost simultaneously. She added, "We came here to…*chat.*"

Greg laughed. "My excuse is better than that. I came to check out the joy in our windows." He walked halfway down the central aisle and looked at Andrew. "I also want to ask you two *sort-of* questions. You didn't actually say that you'd oversee the job of restoring the window." He shrugged. "I suppose you want to think about it before you commit to working for us again. That's probably my fault—but I want you to know that I think you're the right person to help us."

"Thank you, Greg. I don't need to think about anything. I'm ready to begin when you are." Andrew couldn't help but smile at Greg's delighted expression. "What's your second *sort-of* question?"

"We have a small group of stained-glass hobbyists in Glory. It'd be fabulous if you could give us your advice."

"Funny you should say that. I haven't built stained-glass objects myself in years, but I'd love to try my hand again. I used to be pretty good with a soldering iron."

Greg made a sweeping gesture toward the windows in the sanctuary. "Your great-great-great-grandfather really was a wizard."

"I think so, too. But you know—to really observe these windows in all their Glory at night, you have to look at them from the outside."

Greg laughed even louder than before. "I can take a hint."

Andrew watched him leave. When the door clicked shut, he

drew Sharon close to him again. "As I recall, we were…" Before he could kiss her, she kissed him. But only briefly.

"We did come here to chat," she said.

He felt his shoulders slump.

"What's wrong?" she asked. "You suddenly look miserable."

He forced himself to grin. "I'm afraid I'll say the wrong thing and chase you out of my life again."

"But that's not what happened. I chased *you* away. I let you down. I didn't fight hard enough for you. Why…" her voice broke "…why didn't you go home to Asheville?"

Andrew considered his reply. He wanted to get it right. "Every time I thought about it, something held me back. I didn't figure out what that was until yesterday afternoon."

She looked at him, her face full of curiosity. How much of what happened could he tell a pragmatic person like Sharon? Would she doubt the sudden insight he'd experienced? Would she find his conclusions too sappy? He decided to charge ahead.

"I'd been playing with my Bible software, looking for parables that talk about Joy. But then I accidentally stumbled across Ecclesiastes 2:10-11.

"'My heart took delight in all my work, and this was the reward for all my labor. Yet when I surveyed all that my hands had done and what I had toiled to achieve, everything was meaningless, a chasing after the wind, nothing was gained under the sun.'"

He gazed into her eyes. "There it was—my career summed up in a single sentence. A lot of toil that had gained me little. And then I realized that nothing in my life gave me as much delight as when I kissed you and you kissed me back."

He saw her cheeks flush. He grasped her hand and kissed her fingertips.

Andrew went on. "That's when everything dropped into place. *You* are *my* pearl of great value. No aspect of my life is more important to me than you."

She made a soft sound, a moan mixed with a sigh.

"Of course my other relationships failed," he said. "They were doomed from the start, because I've been seeking you—and will never be satisfied by anyone less." He slid closer to her on the pew. "I guess that's why I didn't leave Glory. When a man finds a pearl of great value, he has to understand that finding it is only the beginning. He has to do whatever's necessary to acquire the treasure—that's the get-rid-of-everything-else part—or else he'll lose his treasure.

"I almost lost you by letting my pride get between us. But I've come to my senses. I've disposed of my old baggage. All that matters now are you and me." He wrapped his arms around her again. "I love you more than life itself. And all I can do is hope that you love and need me as much."

He held his breath and waited for her answer. It began with her hand caressing his cheek. "Before I met you, I doubted that I'd ever love another man again. But I love you, and just as important, I trust you. I'm supposed to be the healer in this twosome, but you know what? You've healed my broken heart."

Then came her kiss—a long, lingering kiss that drained the rest of his fear away.

A sudden volley of voices and footsteps in the narthex told Sharon that the abbreviated elders' meeting had ended. "The E.R. is shorthanded during Christmas week," she said "Today was a long day and tomorrow could be worse. I'd better get home."

As she reluctantly extracted herself from Andrew's arms,

she noticed that he'd stopped smiling and seemed oddly pre-occupied—as if he had something left on his plate to complete this evening.

"Did you bike to church?" he asked.

"No. I walked."

"Good!"

His burst of enthusiasm surprised Sharon. Why would he care that she'd walked rather than ridden to the meeting?

He unexpectedly clasped his hands around hers and said, "I have another surprise for you tonight."

"Surprises are good," she murmured.

"However, I need you to trust me."

"I trust you completely." She bent forward and brushed his fingers with her lips. "Even when you act weird."

Although he grinned at Sharon, his mysterious preoccupa-tion had become more visible on his face. "Can we leave the church without meeting a crowd of elders in the narthex?"

"Sure. The choir uses the side entrance after Wednesday night practice." She guided Andrew out the side of the sanctu-ary, past a stairway that rose to the choir loft, and into a corridor that brought them to a metal door equipped with a push bar mechanism. "At this time of night, the door will lock behind us." She stepped aside while he thrust the heavy door shut.

Andrew had parked his SUV in the back of the lot, about fifty paces away from the side entrance. Sharon noted his rented bicycle hanging on the rear rack. When he saw her staring at it, he said, "Wheels of Glory has a bicycle built for two, but it wouldn't fit on the utility rack." He added, "You've gotten me interested in bicycling again."

"It's faster to get around Glory by bike than by car. And it's great exercise."

"Though not entirely painless. My legs have been aching for days—ever since our race to Albemarle Sound."

She was glad that Andrew couldn't see her grimace. "*Um*…there are a few things that happened last week that I'd prefer to forget."

"Like making me weave around rush-hour traffic in the dark, without the benefit of a helmet."

"That's one of them."

He started the engine, and she fastened her seat belt.

They'd traveled for scarcely thirty seconds when Sharon recognized their destination.

"You've brought us back to the waterfront," she said.

"Of course. The Strand is *our* place in Glory." He braked the SUV to a stop. "And there's *our* bench, just as we left it."

"Why come here? It's where we had our first fight."

"Exactly! We need to triumph over that bench—to prove that it can't beat us. It's like getting back on a horse after it throws you."

She laughed. "You are weird."

"And you have to trust me for a few more minutes." Andrew grasped her wrist and tugged her toward him across the vehicle's thick center console.

She jerked her arm free. "My trust is boundless, but there'll be no more hugging or kissing until I get my surprise."

"In that case, woman, out of the SUV. Our bench awaits."

Only after she'd left the SUV did Sharon notice that a dark-colored, full-size sedan had parked a few lengths behind them on The Strand. Its headlights were out, but she could hear the engine idling. And she could make out a murky figure sitting still behind the wheel. Whoever the driver was, he or she was plainly looking their way.

Sharon wasn't prepared for the eruption of dread that coursed through her body that left her starved for breath. Someone had tried to kill Andrew...*twice.* And here he stood in a lonely corner of town at night, with a shadowy stranger skulking nearby.

She moved close to Andrew. "This may sound silly, but I feel...uh, vulnerable near the water tonight. Would you mind if we went someplace else?"

"Vulnerable?" He tapped the tip of her nose with his index finger. "This is the safest place in Glory. We have our own personal police escort. Let's go say hello."

"Oh, my!" Sharon muttered. "I've seen that sedan a thousand times." Her anxiety morphed into chagrin. She'd been spooked by Glory's sole unmarked police cruiser.

Andrew knocked on the driver's side window. An instant later, Angie Ringgold beamed at them. "You guys okay?" she asked.

"We're good," Sharon replied. "We came here to look at the water."

Andrew gave an exaggerated shake of his head, and then said to Angie, "Isn't it a crime for a civilian to lie to the police?"

She poked Andrew in his ribs with her elbow.

Angie snickered. "It's a fine night for looking—or *whatever.* Clear skies and not too cold."

Sharon abruptly realized that Ty Keefe hadn't been following her, after all. He'd arranged for the Glory Police to trail Andrew, hoping to prevent another attempt on his life.

She uttered a purposeful sigh at the unfairness of it all. Who would want to murder Andrew Ballantine—the man who'd single-handedly stopped the window war at Glory Community Church, the man who successfully advocated the importance of joy to the assembled elders, the man she'd fallen hopelessly in love with?

Angie waved at Andrew. "I've determined that everything is under control on Glory's waterfront." She aimed another salute at Sharon, and then rolled her window shut. A few seconds later she drove the cruiser away.

Andrew walked on the grassy strip and stopped next to the bench.

Now what? Sharon thought as she sat down. But instead of joining her, Andrew dropped to one knee. "Consider the strange effects of this town on my heart, Nurse Pickard," he said. "Someone tried to stop my heart with oleander toxin. I've had a major change of heart regarding a historic stained-glass window. And my heart came close to breaking when you and I allowed circumstances to pull us apart." He took her hand gently and rested her palm on his chest. "There's only one way I can be sure of a steady *thump, thump, thump* during the years to come. You'll have to marry me."

Sharon heard a gasp and knew that she had made the sibilant noise. *You can't keep doing that!* She was a nurse, a professional trained to deal with events that staggered other people. It was no excuse that Andrew repeatedly caused shock waves that disrupted her breathing.

That's why he'd seemed pensive earlier. He was busy choosing the words that would shake your world.

"Now that I've found my Pearl of Great Value," he continued, "I want you with me forever." He rose to his feet and pulled her along with him, "I want to marry you, Sharon. Do you want to marry me?"

The utter directness of his question—its total simplicity—generated another seismic tremor in her innards. She'd never contemplated marrying Andrew.

Don't say you need time to think about it. That's wimp-speak.

He gazed at her, searching her expression in the orange light spilling from the nearby streetlamp. "I know I've surprised you. Some people might think we haven't known each other long enough to fall in love. I'm sure you need time to think about everything I've said."

"Says who?" She reached up and touched his cheek. "I love you, too. Andrew. I knew that back in the gazebo. Of course I'll marry you."

This time Andrew gasped. "You've made me happier than I can say." His voice choked. "I may start jumping up and down again."

"Me, too." She laughed. "I'll enjoy being a pearl on a pedestal."

"*Uh-uh.* That's the old cartoon."

"No more pedestal?"

He shook his head. "No pedestal. Just lots of joy."

He kissed her for what seemed an eternity.

SEVENTEEN

Sharon put her arms around Andrew. "I never actually said that I'd go tonight. I distinctly remember leaving my acceptance up in the air." She felt him kiss the top of her head.

"You didn't say yes, but I did." He kissed her again. "And because the news of our engagement has traveled the length and breadth of Glory, Amanda will expect both of us to attend her before-church reception. Like it or not, you have to accompany me to The Robert Burns Inn." He kissed her a third time. "It's Christmas Eve."

"Stop mussing my hair. You'll make me look as bad-tempered as I feel." She stepped a pace backward. "I'm good around difficult people, but Amanda brings out the worst in me."

Andrew reached out and patted her hair; she slapped his hand.

"Amanda's not so bad," he said. "She wants to be friendly— but goes about it the wrong way. Keep telling yourself that and you'll learn to like her eventually."

She tried to shrug off Andrew's comment, but she knew that he was right. She'd have to cope with Amanda Turner, who was destined to become a prominent resident in Glory—one of Emma's business colleagues and a likely member of Glory Community Church.

"Okay..." Sharon grumbled. "I'll stop being judgmental about her, but if she flirts with you at the reception, she'll get a different kind of Christmas punch from me."

Andrew laughed. "I love you, too."

She scooted into her downstairs half bathroom to check her makeup and discovered that she looked unmistakably joyous. She hadn't stopped grinning since Andrew had proposed. Without thinking about it, she brought her left hand close to her chin and flicked her fingers. Her new engagement ring sparkled in the mirror like a constellation and filled her with delight. Andrew had insisted on going to Glorious Jewelry that morning. The shop had the perfect ring in stock and agreed to size it on the spot. Why even try to hide how she felt? It had been ages since she'd experienced such a barrage of happiness.

She found Andrew holding her coat, ready to help her put it on. The simple gesture made her teary. She sniffed.

"Oh, oh! Did I do something wrong?"

"You reminded me that I expected to be alone during the holidays. But now I have you."

"A man who brings tears to your eyes." He smiled. "You're as weird as I am."

"We deserve one another."

They found Campbell Street The Robert Burns Inn over-flowing with cars and vans. The small parking lot behind the inn was nearly full; Andrew managed to back the SUV into a small space near the far corner.

"Amanda must have invited half of Glory to her Christmas Eve bash," he said. "And I cringe at the thought of her next electric bill."

Sharon looked through the SUV's windshield at the multiple strings of lights—and glowing wreaths—that filled the inn's back garden. Emma had hung some Christmas lights at the Captain, but nothing like this display.

"This reception could become an annual event in Glory," she said. "Evening at the Bobby Burns then a candlelight worship service at church."

"I hear a Christmas carol." He slipped out of his seat and hurried around the SUV to open Sharon's door. "It sounds like Amanda hired professional singers."

Sharon looped her arm through Andrew's. She heard the lyrics—"Ding Dong! Merrily on High"—to one of her favorite carols wafting on the cold crisp air. Andrew had heard right; the voices sounded professional. Amanda was clearly determined to impress the townsfolk of Glory with her refurbished B and B.

She's certainly impressed me.

"Shall we go in?" Sharon tipped her head toward the inn's back door.

"Not that way," Andrew said. "I'm escorting the best-looking woman in Glory, tonight. We'll make our grand entrance through the front door."

Sharon walked a step behind Andrew on the stone path that led around the side of the two-story building. The Bobby Burns didn't have a front porch and seemed smaller to her than The Scottish Captain. Once inside, though, she found that both the parlor and the dining room were larger.

Sharon felt uneasy being among the first to tread on the parlor's new sculptured wall-to-wall carpeting. Andrew guessed her thoughts. "I hope she makes her guests take off their shoes."

About twenty partygoers were gathered inside the parlor, sitting on a varied collection of sofas and occasional chairs, all modern in design—all, Sharon presumed, pricey in upholstery.

A gas log burned in the fireplace along the back wall, the flames reflecting in numerous gilded mirrors strategically positioned around the room. Scores of lit candles atop the parlor's table-tops added to the warm light and filled the space with enticing aromas. Someone with a careful eye for detail had hung framed prints and watercolors on the walls with great care. Amanda or her decorator had made it seem that the furnishings had adorned this room forever.

An equally artistic designer had created the Christmas tree that stood in the far corner. It was small, only six feet high, but exquisitely decorated with handblown iridescent ornaments that must have cost Amanda a fortune.

While Sharon examined the tree, Andrew took a closer look at a large stained-glass panel that hung above the fireplace. It was illuminated from behind by a light box installed in the wall—another significant investment in décor.

"The cartoon depicts wildflowers of Scotland," Andrew said to her. "The crimson flower is a Bloody Cranesbill. The big blue blossom is a Meadow Cranesbill."

Sharon took over. "My turn, smarty-pants. The pink flowers are a spray of heather and the bunch of yellow flowers are Primrose."

Andrew jumped back in. "And the purple flower on the tall stalk is the inevitable thistle, the symbol of Scotland." He concluded, "I'm impressed—the panel is more tasteful than most decorative stained-glass objects."

"I'm so glad the glass guru is satisfied." She winked at him. "Let's say hello to our hostess."

"Welcome! Welcome!" Amanda cooed, from her perch on a tall stool next to the kitchen counter. "It's such a treat to see you both! I've heard your news." She slipped off the stool, hugged Andrew and patted Sharon's shoulder. She made a show of dabbing her eyes, although Sharon couldn't see any signs of actual crying. "I'm a *hopeless* romantic." Amanda swiped away an imaginary tear. "I snivel at engagements and positively sob at weddings. I can't help myself."

Amanda began to point at Sharon's left hand. "Look at that gorgeous ring! Show me! Show me! Show me!"

Sharon glared at Andrew, who seemed not to mind that Amanda's voice was loud enough to be heard everywhere in the inn. In no time at all, other guests came into the kitchen to check out her ring.

"Let me assure you," Amanda said, "that Mr. Harrison Turner will be in serious trouble when I see him again. He gave me a measly diamond chip that I am too embarrassed to wear in public."

Sharon was taken aback. *What game was Amanda playing at?* What did she accomplish by publicly belittling her husband? No wonder poor Harrison traveled a lot.

Amanda made a broad gesture that encompassed most of the inn. "Enough grim talk about me. Feel free to wander everywhere on the first floor. The guest rooms on the second are not quite ready for prime time yet."

Sharon stalked out of the kitchen. How could anyone not be judgmental about Amanda Turner? Emma might be stuck with her as fellow B and B owner, but she had no reason to "cope" with Amanda—except perhaps Jesus' admonition to love your neighbor.

There must be an Amanda loophole somewhere in Scripture.

Sharon and Andrew found Emma and Rafe in the library, a guest lounge to-be currently filled with mostly empty bookcases. Sharon saw the bulge under Rafe's jacket and realized that he'd come armed. Rafe was more than an ordinary guest this evening; he was also here to protect Andrew.

"What do you think of the new and improved Robert Burns Inn?" Sharon asked Emma.

"I think that Amanda will be a fearsome competitor. She's spent a ton of money to spruce up the place. The downstairs is grand and I expect the guest rooms will be equally opulent. Guests will love the Bobby Burns." She almost smiled. "I'll have to make sure that the Captain is up to the challenge."

"You don't know the half of it, Emma," Rex Grainger said as he strode into the library looking exceedingly pleased with himself. Sharon wondered how Andrew would react to Rex— but he shook the editor's hand without showing a hint of anger.

I've got to learn that trick when I'm around Amanda.

"I hear you've suggested a window compromise that we all can live with. I told the elders that they should pay attention to you. I'm glad they finally listened to me," Rex said to Andrew. "By the way—we need to talk some more, so that I can fully understand your recommendations. The people of Glory have a right to know what will happen at Glory Community Church."

Andrew ignored Rex's pomposity and changed the subject. "You were about to give Emma some advice."

"Indeed I was!" He moved within whispering distance to Emma and said softly, "I have it on good authority that Amanda bought large quantities of commercial carpeting—far more than she needed for this inn. The obvious conclusion is that Amanda plans to redecorate other properties when she acquires them." He added a soft snicker. "I'm convinced that she plans to build a B and B empire in this corner of North Carolina. You'd better watch your step, Emma. Amanda may have the Captain in her sights."

Sharon noted that neither Emma nor Andrew seemed surprised by Rex's revelation. Sharon knew that competition in the commercial marketplace could be as cutthroat as a shooting war. She often treated the frontline casualties—businesspeople who arrived in the E.R. with stress-related heart attacks, ulcers and breakdowns. She hoped that Emma would never be "wounded" doing battle against the other B and Bs in Glory.

Sharon and Andrew continued their tour of the downstairs. When they reached the inn's central hallway, a tray of red-colored drinks floated past them on the arm of Debbie Akers, a soprano in the Glory Community Church choir, and a student at Glory High School. Sharon guessed that Amanda had hired her to help tonight, probably at Emma's suggestion. She often used Debbie to supplement her tiny staff. The last time Sharon had seen Debbie was at the Captain's tea party. She'd distributed different kinds of tea cakes.

"What are you serving?" Sharon asked.

"Cranberry juice."

Sharon took two glasses and handed one to Andrew. "Cranberry juice isn't sweet. It's safe for you to drink tonight."

He made a face. "I don't accept that I may be in danger at a Christmas Eve party surrounded by people I know."

"I don't think you're in danger, either, but now that I've got you, I intend to keep you. Unpoisoned!"

He didn't exactly smile at her, but Sharon could tell that he was pleased by her concern.

"The guests seem to be gathering in the parlor," he said. "Let's join them."

They entered through one door as Amanda entered through the other pushing a cart of food. This must have been a pre-arranged signal, because Daniel Hartman stood up and said, "Amanda has asked me to say the first prayer spoken in the refurbished Bobby Burns Inn.

"Heavenly Father, tonight we remember what Your angelic host said to humble shepherds more than two millennia ago— Glory to God in the highest, and on earth peace to men on whom his favor rests.

"What can be more appropriate than to pray that this B and B is always a place of shalom—body, mind and spirit—for the guests who will stay here in the years to come.

"We ask Your blessing on the food we are about to enjoy. Give us grateful hearts for the many bounties we receive from You.

"And if we may be so bold, we also pray—along with Amanda—that this inn will be full in the future…not unlike the inn in Bethlehem where Your precious Son was born. In Jesus' name we pray."

Amanda spoke the first amen; others joined in quickly.

A few seconds later, Sharon heard Emma, who was standing behind her, mutter, "Oh, dear! Amanda has a lot to learn about the hospitality business."

"Really? What didn't I see her do wrong?"

"There's a plate full of peeled shrimp on that cart. I just watched Amanda eat three of them."

"Why is that bad?"

"It's poor form for an innkeeper to eat food that's likely to be in short supply until her guests have had their fill."

Sharon knew that she'd never forget this moment in time— the instant when the pieces fell together in place in her mind. She felt a gust of relief blow through her body. Now that she knew who wanted to kill Andrew, he'd never be in danger again. Not with her glued to his side.

She tugged on Andrew's sleeve and guided him into a space between the Christmas tree and the wall. "You ate two helpings of Strathbogie Mist before you got sick, didn't you?"

"I told you that in the hospital."

"You also told me that Emma Neilson gave you the second helping?"

"Correct. She placed it in front of me when you and I were chatting. We were standing near a small table inside the gazebo. After I ate the second helping, we decided to get away from the crowd, so we moved to the gazebo's stairs. I began to feel sick a few minutes later."

"Boy. Talk about being clever. Oleander toxin is a great poison to use at a social event, like a tea party…or before a church gathering."

"What do you mean by that?"

"All will be clear if you let me think out loud—about what happened to you at the tea party."

"What do you want me to do?"

"Listen, without talking." She placed her finger across his lips. "Cardiac rhythm problems are tough to diagnose. There's an excellent chance of getting them wrong. I know of more than thirty potentially fatal diseases that trigger the same kind of heart troubles as oleandrin." She squeezed his right hand between hers. "You were lucky when you arrived at the E.R."

"Lucky? I was half dead."

"True, but when the paramedics brought you in, you presented the classic symptoms of cardiac glycoside poisoning.

That's why Ken Lehman put you through the right battery of tests. He diagnosed oleander poisoning in a matter of minutes. Many diagnoses take much longer than that.

"You were also lucky that I was standing next to you when you got sick, and that Dr. Haley Carroll recognized the severity of your symptoms. What would have happened if you'd merely put yourself to bed with the idea of sleeping off what you figured was a bout of food poisoning?"

"Nothing good, I presume?"

"You'd have been dead the next morning, and everyone might have chalked it up to a fatal heart attack at an unusually young age."

"I hope you're finished thinking aloud. You're giving me what my mother used to call the heebie-jeebies."

Sharon saw Amanda approaching, carrying a pair of colorful Christmas cups, covered with red, green and silver elves.

"Young lovers always hide in the corner," Amanda said with a teasing smile. "And poor hostesses must continuously work to keep them part of the party." She moaned pitifully to emphasize her plight. "Emma wants to deliver a toast with hot chocolate. She asked me to bring everyone a cup."

Amanda offered the tray, and Sharon took the pair of cups. Amanda circled back toward the door that led to the kitchen.

Sharon studied the contents. Hot chocolate was more than sweet enough to disguise the taste of oleandrin. She touched her pinkie into the cup and tasted the drop of hot chocolate with the tip of her tongue.

Slightly bitter.

Emma walked to the middle of the parlor. "I'd like to welcome our newest innkeeper to Glory, and also thank her for this lovely reception. Let's raise our cups to Amanda Turner."

More than twenty cups moved upward, all of them decorated with gold and silver angels.

Andrew touched Sharon's arm. "I need one of those cups you're holding."

"No you don't!" she said loud enough to startle Andrew and end the other conversations beginning in the parlor. All eyes turned to Sharon.

Sharon stepped forward. "You'll excuse me for not joining in Emma's fine toast, or for not letting Andrew drink from either of these cups," she addressed the guests. "You see…our cups are different than yours. Different pictures on the outside, different contents on the inside. Our hot chocolate contains oleandrin—a deadly poison.

"The different designs made it easy to tell the tainted cups apart from the cups full of ordinary hot chocolate. Didn't they, Amanda?"

She locked eyes with the maligned hostess. The room filled with murmurs. Amanda silenced them when she leveled a finger at Sharon and said, "You ungrateful skunk. I invite you to my home and you make wild accusations."

"Wild? Not at all. You also poisoned Andrew at the tea party Emma threw at The Scottish Captain."

She heard Andrew move behind her. She held out her hand to stop him.

"That's ridiculous," Amanda said. "Why would I want to poison Andrew?"

"The first time around you didn't. But when Andrew became an accidental victim at Emma Neilson's tea party, you decided to kill him to shift suspicion away from you. You sent Andrew poisoned chocolate cherries last week, and tonight you served us poisoned hot chocolate."

Amanda gave a forced laugh. "Accidental victim. Tainted chocolates. Poisoned hot chocolate. You must be losing your mind."

"I admit that it took me quite awhile to figure things out, Amanda, to understand The Scottish Captain is your pearl of great value." She raised a brow. "The merchant in the parable was prepared to give up everything he owned to acquire his pearl. You were prepared to commit murder to get hold of The Scottish Captain."

"Nonsense! You're spouting nonsense!"

"Last summer, a convenient heart attack—suffered by poor Bill Dorsey—made it possible for you to acquire The Robert Burns Inn for much less than it was worth." She sighed. "Your scheme worked so well, you decided to try it again. Perhaps another convenient heart attack would get you The Scottish Captain at a distress-sale price?"

Emma Neilson began to cough.

"You can drink your hot chocolate," Sharon said. "It's okay—tonight."

"She tried to poison me," Emma sputtered, "but I gave my dish of Strathbogie Mist to Andrew."

Sharon nodded. "You were determined to be a classy inn-keeper. When you saw Andrew scarf down his first helping, you offered him yours as a second helping. You wanted to make sure your guest had his fill."

Amanda's expression had changed. Her confidence was gone, replaced by a look of pure terror.

"You can't prove any of this," she seethed.

"No, but I'm sure that Special Agent Tyrone Keefe, of the North Carolina State Bureau of Investigation, will find a mountain of evidence once he starts looking into your life."

192 Season of Glory

Amanda suddenly threw the tray full of angel cups she was holding. It smashed into the Christmas tree, smashing dozens of ornaments and spattering hot chocolate on most of the brand-new furniture and carpeting. She ran out of the parlor. A moment later Sharon heard an engine start, and a car screech out of the parking lot.

All eyes turned again, this time to Rafe. He shrugged. "By running, she helped Ty Keefe build the case against her. And where can she go? We'll find her in a day or two."

Sharon felt Andrew's arm snake around her. "I can't make up my mind," he said. "Do I thank you, or kiss you first?"

Everyone in the room shouted, "Kiss her!"

EIGHTEEN

On this jaunt through Glory, Andrew found that Sharon couldn't out-pedal him. The new bicycle she'd given him for Christmas was a touring model with a strong, lightweight frame, a comfortable seat and a smooth-as-silk gear shifter. He easily kept up with her as she wove from street to street. And his new helmet, complete with a flip-out rearview mirror, increased his confidence.

They'd decided to follow the scenic route back to The Scottish Captain—a journey that included a two-mile-long bicycle path along the Albemarle Sound shoreline. Andrew didn't notice much Carolinian scenery because he couldn't help staring at Sharon as she pedaled a few yards ahead of him. He'd met this beautiful and talented woman less than two weeks ago. And now they were engaged to be married—a pair of no-nonsense people brought together by an incredible chain of events.

God definitely has a sense of humor. And dramatically different notions about correct timing. Who could argue that their whirlwind courtship hadn't produced the perfect outcome?

He accelerated alongside Sharon and outdid her smile with a bigger one of his own. Downtown Glory lay ahead of them, the traffic unusually heavy for a Thursday afternoon. But this was no ordinary Thursday. It was the day after Christmas, one of the busiest shopping days of the year in the U.S. And in many other English-speaking countries it was *Boxing Day*.

Leave it to Emma Neilson to come up with a Boxing Day Open House "to celebrate the engagement of my two favorite lovers of Scottish tradition."

Both Andrew's and Sharon's grandparents had celebrated Boxing Day when they were kids. The tradition was said to hark back to feudal times when the Lord and Lady of the manor distributed boxes of expensive necessities to their workers: spices, tools, meats, cloth and dried foods. The giving of boxes to one's employees became "Boxing Day," a national holiday in many English-speaking countries.

"Be here at three-thirty," Emma had said when she'd invited him during breakfast. "It's a completely informal get-together. Come as you are."

Andrew downshifted his bicycle and murmured, "We'll soon see if Emma meant it." His new biking outfit—another of Sharon's gifts—was the epitome of informality.

The morning had been lovely, much warmer than the season, like many winter mornings in North Carolina. Cycling pants, long-sleeved jerseys and light jackets had been all the clothing they needed. They'd spent the day out and around Glory making plans for their future. Everything they thought about seemed to drop into place.

Where would they live? In Glory, of course. Sharon was delighted to be working at Glory Regional Hospital and Andrew could live anywhere. "Glory will be a great name on my business cards."

Wedding plans? More easy decisions. They'd be married in Glory Community Church, with Daniel Hartman officiating.

Their honeymoon? In Scotland, of course. They wouldn't gaze at a single Scottish stained-glass church window, but they'd definitely visit the ancestral homes of the Pickards and the Ballantines.

Church work? The elders, talking among themselves after the Monday night meeting, had decided to dissolve the WinReC now that a practical restoration strategy was in place. Ann Trask Miller and Andrew would share the job of hiring an artist and selecting a firm to build the window. "Your window work is done," Daniel had told Sharon. "Now you can start singing again."

Andrew and Sharon made a graceful side-by-side left turn onto Osborn Street and continued to Broad Street. When they'd locked their bikes to the rack near The Captain's front porch, he drew her into his arms. "How about a Boxing Day kiss before we go inside?"

"Only one?"

"I love you," he whispered in her ear.

"I love you back," she murmured in reply.

"I wish I could hold you like this forever."

"Not me." She broke loose from his hug. "I'm hungry… and thirsty."

He laughed. "Actually, I am too." He took her hand and ushered her up the steps to the front door.

"The two *Scotophiles* have arrived," he said.

"Rafe and I are in the kitchen," Emma called back.

"How's the happy couple today?" Rafe asked as Andrew pushed through the swinging door.

"Still getting used to being a couple," Sharon answered.

Emma used the opportunity of Sharon's distraction to give Andrew a thumbs-up sign. Good! Everything was arranged as he, Emma and Rafe had planned.

"We still have an hour until the other guests begin to arrive," Rafe said. "Emma will set out some snacks and I will break all my department's rules by telling you everything that Ty Keefe told me about Amanda Turner."

He smiled at Sharon. "You deserve to know, but I'm counting on you not to snitch. Ty is much bigger than me."

"It's a deal." She blew Rafe a kiss, then sat down at the kitchen table next to Andrew.

Rafe rocked his chair backward so that it rested on its rear legs. "Well, as has been reported nonstop for the past twenty-four hours on TV, the North Carolina State Highway Patrol caught up with Amanda on Route 301, a few miles this side of the South Carolina border. Once Ty got her talking, she didn't stop.

"Ty confirmed everything that Sharon deduced—with a few additions. It seems likely that Bill Dorsey didn't die from a routine heart attack. He succumbed several hours after the Dorseys hosted a backyard barbecue for the Bobby Burns's guests. Amanda was one of those guests—a rather telling coincidence that no one noticed before."

Sharon and Andrew urged him to continue.

"When Amanda checked into the Bobby Burns, she told Carol Dorsey that she'd come to Glory to find a good business opportunity, a scarily true statement." Rafe rebalanced his chair. "Ty has asked us to take a close look at Bill Dorsey's medical records. We also have *other* options should we decide we need them, like exhuming."

Andrew glanced at Sharon. They'd both understood what Rafe meant and felt glad that he hadn't gone into detail.

Rafe went on. "After Amanda purchased The Robert Burns Inn, she decided to try the same strategy again. Why not? It had worked flawlessly the first time around. No one, not even Carol Dorsey, had suspected foul play."

Sharon's heart ached for Bill's family and she prayed that someone bringing his killer to justice would help bring her some semblance of peace.

"A few drops of oleander toxin poisoned Bill, and then Carol Dorsey sold her spouse's B and B for a song," Rafe confirmed. "Amanda was counting on me doing the same thing. She figured that with Emma dead, I'd want out of the bed-and-breakfast business and would be happy to sell the Captain to the first bidder." Rafe brought his chair forward with a thump. "She was right. I would have decided to sell."

Emma snorted. "You'd walk away so quickly after all the work I put into the place?"

"Sorry, my love, but I'm a policeman, not an innkeeper. Carol Dorsey couldn't face the task by herself, and neither could I on my own."

Emma became pensive. "Amanda Turner is an evil woman. She counted on Carol and you behaving that way. It gives me the shivers to think that I felt sorry for her, that I trusted her, that I made her a guest under our roof." She spoke slowly, plainly annoyed. "At a significantly discounted room rate."

"Ah, yes. You reminded me of an important point. Amanda didn't become our guest by accident, or out of necessity. The redecoration work at the Bobby Burns was finished two weeks ago, but then Amanda heard about the tea party, apparently from Debbie Akers. That's why she wanted to spend a few nights at the Captain."

He exhaled sharply. "As Sharon deduced, Amanda considered a late-evening social gathering as a perfect occasion to poison someone with oleandrin. If she was lucky, the victim would die in his or her sleep, significantly reducing the risk of discovery."

"Aren't you forgetting something important?" Andrew asked. "Amanda was at the tea party. She must have seen Emma give me the tainted dessert. She stood by and let a stranger be poisoned—all because Emma was a good hostess."

Sharon pretended to jab her fork at Andrew. "No! It was gluttony that nearly did you in. You were poisoned because you wolfed down *two* ramekins of Strathbogie Mist, when some guests didn't even enjoy one helping."

"What choice did I have? It was such delicious Strathbogie Mist."

Sharon groaned.

"I'm not exaggerating by much. I look forward to a lifetime of truly fabulous Scottish desserts."

Emma chimed in. "Amanda meant to poison me, but accidentally poisoned Andrew. Why try a second, and a third time to kill him?"

"That was Ty Keefe's fault," Rafe said. "He frightened Amanda when he interviewed her. He seemed determined to find out what happened—and he hadn't arrested Sharon. Amanda was worried that NCSBI's spotlight would eventually fall on her. The police might discover a link between B and B owners and cardiac poisons, but she had absolutely no motive for killing Andrew. Killing him would keep Ty's attention on Sharon."

Emma suddenly spoke. "I have to know! Did Amanda get her poison from the oleander bush in our backyard?"

Rafe shook his head. "Thankfully, no. She arrived in Glory with a bottle of oleander toxin she'd brewed up in her mother's house in Florida."

"That makes sense," Sharon said. "Amanda probably didn't know who she'd want to kill, so she came to town fully prepared."

Andrew raised his hand. "Maybe I'm naive to ask, but how does one surreptitiously add oleander toxin to Strathbogie Mist? Is Amanda some sort of magician or sleight-of-hand artist?"

"Neither," Rafe said. "She simply poured the stuff into the ceramic ramekin and slid the dish next to Emma. People at a party are too busy chatting and shmoozing to notice that sort of thing."

"Well, I certainly didn't notice," Andrew said. "Do you know how she poisoned the chocolate truffles?"

"She used a 'glue injector' she bought at Hobbies of Glory. It's a gadget intended to squirt glue into the joints of model airplanes. But that came later—after you survived your first dose of oleandrin."

"It sounds so bizarre," Sharon said. "Death by Strathbogie Mist."

"Amanda had lots of dishes to choose from at Emma's tea party, but she had to work quickly. According to Ty, Amanda had three criteria. First, as Sharon pointed out, the food had to be sweet enough to cover the bitterness of oleandrin. Second, it had to be something that Emma would eat. And third, the food had to be prepared—or delivered—by a person who'd seem a good suspect to the police, if the police ever discovered the real cause of death."

Andrew saw Sharon make a face. "Not that that was likely," she said. "She presumed that Glory's careless medical establishment would decide that Emma had an ordinary heart attack—much like Bill Dorsey."

She took an exasperated swat at the table. "Another overworked B and B owner bites the dust!"

"Yes and no," Rafe said. "Amanda *hoped* that Emma's death would be written off to natural causes, but she feared that the police would conduct a thorough investigation. After all, Emma was considerably younger than Bill. And Rafe is Deputy Chief of Police. So Amanda decided that she needed a candidate in the wings—someone the police would consider a viable suspect."

"Someone like me," Sharon said.

Rafe nodded. "Amanda was astonished that Ty Keefe didn't arrest you immediately."

"I was, too." Sharon wrung her hands. "If I ever get my hands on that woman…"

"You had poor Ty Keefe bouncing back and forth. His detective's instinct told him that you didn't poison Andrew, but the circumstantial evidence kept clamoring that you did."

Rafe grinned. "You'll be happy to know that Ty is now fully satisfied that you're innocent. He's also a tad embarrassed. It's not often that a prime suspect solves the case."

Andrew felt curious enough to ask another question. "Why didn't Amanda try to implicate Calvin Constable? He'd be a better suspect than Sharon. 'Bitter breakfast chef gets back at B and B owner by poisoning guest at tea party.'"

"I know why," Emma said. "Good breakfast chefs are pearls of great value in their own right. She wanted to hire Calvin, not send him to prison."

Rafe twirled his right index finger, a summing-up gesture. "And so we finish our simple tale of a murderous woman, consumed by greed, and determined to become the B and B czarina of eastern North Carolina—at any cost."

"Before you sign off," Emma said, "where did Amanda's money come from? She seems to have plenty—to buy B and Bs and make lavish improvements."

"I wasn't going to mention this because it's going on in another jurisdiction, but the police in Birmingham, Alabama, are looking into the accidental death three years ago of a wealthy man named Harrison Turner."

"Amanda's husband back in Alabama?"

"Her *late* husband. He supposedly fell off a bass boat and drowned."

"No doubt because he refused to eat the sweet foods she'd prepared for him," Andrew quipped.

Sharon groaned again. "I may be forced to rethink our engagement."

Andrew saw Emma wink at him. *Time to begin.*

"So Andrew," Emma said, "what did Sharon give you for Christmas?"

"A new bicycle. And these…" He stood up and did a slow pirouette to model his biking outfit.

"So few men look good in tights," Rafe said with an appropriate sneer.

"What can I say?" Andrew said drolly. "Good looks are in my genes."

Rafe threw a canapé at Andrew. "Try one. Calvin Constable invented them in honor of Boxing Day. Miniature roast beef in Yorkshire pudding."

Emma turned to Sharon. "What did Andrew give you for Christmas?"

"He hasn't had a chance to go shopping. His proposal of marriage—and my engagement ring—were quite enough."

"Not enough for me," Andrew said.

"What do you—"

Emma cut Sharon off. "Look next to the refrigerator."

Andrew helped Sharon slide a large corrugated cardboard box to the center of the kitchen floor. It made tinkling and rattling noises as they pushed it.

She yanked the top flaps open and looked inside. "What on earth?"

"I wouldn't unpack that—you'll never get all the pieces back inside. It's a complete stained-glass tool kit. Everything you need to build full-scale projects."

"Everything *I* need?"

"Well, I assumed that you'd attend the stained-glass course I plan to teach at Glory Community College."

"Me?"

"Naturally my new wife will want to take an interest in a subject I care about deeply."

"Don't push it, unless you intend to learn how to tie sutures and insert intravenous needles."

"Hmm. I see your point."

He took Sharon in his arms and kissed her until Rafe said, "Boy, that was clever. He gave her the Christmas present he wanted."

Andrew heard Sharon laughing. He began to laugh even louder.

EPILOGUE

From the June 15 edition of the Glory Gazette:

PICKARD-BALLANTINE WEDDING
INAUGURATES A RESTORED SANCTUARY

Glory, North Carolina. It goes without saying that
the bride was beautiful and the women standing up
with the bride stunning. What made the nuptials of
Sharon Pickard and Andrew Ballantine at Glory Community Church especially unusual was that all the
men in the wedding party looked dazzling in their
authentic Scottish kilts. Reverend Dr. Daniel Hartman
(also wearing a kilt) officiated.

The bride is the daughter of David and Nathalie
Pickard of Charlotte, North Carolina. The groom is
the son of Webster and Elizabeth Ballantine of Knoxville, Tennessee.

The bride and groom walked down the aisle
together, led by a Scottish bagpiper. The groom's

best man was Gordon Pollack of Glory. Standing up with the bride were Emma Neilson and Katherine (Kate) Neilson, both of Glory.

A reception after the wedding was held at The Scottish Captain. The guests enjoyed traditional Scottish dishes—including cock-a-leeky soup, finnan haddie and haggis—prepared by Calvin Constable, the inn's chef.

The Pickard-Ballantine nuptials was the first wedding ceremony held in Glory Community's fully restored sanctuary. The new, painted, stained-glass window (the original was destroyed in a fire last year) illustrates the New Testament parable of *The Pearl of Great Value*. The focal point of the replacement window, designed by Frances Brewer of New Bern, is the joyous merchant who seems to smile at everyone in the sanctuary.

This reporter found the joyous motif wholly appropriate for a joyous day.

FAMED STAINED-GLASS CONSULTANT MOVES TO GLORY

Andrew Ballantine Consulting, LLC, one of the world's leading consultants on stained-glass church windows, has relocated its offices from Asheville, North Carolina, to the third floor of the Glory National Bank building. The space, formerly occupied by the Scottish Heritage Society, became available when the Society purchased The Robert Burns Inn on Campbell Street. The first floor of the "Bobby

Burns" will be transformed into a Scottish Heritage museum and the second floor used for staff offices and meeting rooms.

* * * * *

Dear Reader,

If there's a single word we had in mind when we wrote *Season of Glory,* our fourth novel set in Glory, North Carolina, that word is "joy."

Sharon Pickard and Andrew Ballantine eventually experience:

- The joy of the Christmas season
- The joy of falling in love
- The joy of a job well done
- Even the joy of understanding a passage of Scripture that many others find baffling

But note the word "eventually." Sharon and Andrew begin the ten days before this particular Christmas in Glory with a surprisingly short supply of joy. Their *enjoyments* are interrupted by their past relationships, by circumstances beyond their control…and by the malicious actions of a joyless poisoner.

Alas, although our story is fiction, many people find it difficult to enjoy the Christmas season—sometimes because they haven't found their "pearl of great value," the thing they want most in the world.

Jesus' parable of *The Pearl of Great Value* plays a central role in this novel. There are so many different interpretations out there (we included several of the most popular in the novel) that many Christians feel confused by the story. We liked the mystery inherent in the parable, and also its relevance to the tale we told.

The simple truth is that it can be difficult to see what really should matter most in life. It's easy to recognize that the poisoner was wrong to be willing to kill someone to acquire something of value. But what about Andrew's notion that he had a duty to protect the "artistic and historic integrity" of James's Ballantine stained-glass window, no matter what the personal cost to him? Many people, perhaps you and we, might think that he was right. It turned out he wasn't.

Speaking for everyone in Glory, Merry Christmas and Happy New Year!

Ron and Janet Benrey

QUESTIONS FOR DISCUSSION

1. The parables of Jesus teach us how we should live by the examples they give. Which is your favorite parable? What does it teach you? And how does it affect your faith journey?

2. What does *The Pearl of Great Value* parable mean to you? Like the congregation at Glory Community Church, do you struggle with the meaning of this particular parable? Who do you go to for guidance when discussing a difficult Bible passage?

3. Sharon was asked to help her church by serving on a committee. We are often asked to serve on various committees. Do you always say yes and regret your answer at a later date? Or are you selective about what you choose to do, saying yes only to those things you know you will enjoy?

4. Sharon Pickard was forced to fire the man she loved by telling him he was no longer needed. Have you ever held a position of authority in which you were forced to fire someone you liked? How did you handle it? How did it turn out?

5. Andrew Ballantine thought he knew what was best for everyone. Have you ever thought you knew what was best only to find out later that someone else had a better idea?

6. In *Season of Glory,* a child's fresh eye uncovered a truth that we tried to convey to adults through his drawing. Sometimes children hit the nail on the head with their

answers to our questions. How do you respond when this happens? Do you listen, or do you dismiss the idea?

7. Sooner or later we will all face an illness. We expect to live, and to recover with proper care. But has anyone put your life in peril the way Andrew was threatened? How did you respond? Were you able to forgive them?

8. We all love to be loved. We pray that God will send us the right mate when the time is right. Have you been able to wait patiently for the man or woman God chose for you? How did you deal with the passage of time?

9. Sharon loves Andrew and he loves her, but he was prepared to walk away and she was prepared to let him. What would you do to hold on to the person you love more than any other? Would you fight to keep them, or let them go if that's what you thought they wanted?

10. Have you ever wanted something badly enough that you would do almost anything to get it, like the poisoner in this story? What strength did you call upon to resist the temptation to take what you wanted, even if it was not offered to you? How did you handle your disappointment? Did you grow emotionally as a result of not getting what you wanted when you wanted it?

11. Sharon has a great friend in Emma. Do you have someone in your life with whom you share your problems? Is this person a family member or a friend?

12. Sharon became a suspect in a serious crime. All she had to defend herself with was the truth. Have you ever been accused by authorities of doing something you know you didn't do? How did you handle it? To whom did you turn for help? Did your friends stand by you?

13. *Season of Glory* takes place at Christmastime. What particular tradition do you enjoy that helps you celebrate the true season of glory?

* * * * *

And now, turn the page for a sneak preview of
WHAT SARAH SAW by Margaret Daley,
the first story in WITHOUT A TRACE,
the exciting new continuity
from Love Inspired Suspense!
On sale in January 2009
from Steeple Hill Books.

PROLOGUE

A patrol car was parked on Main Street in front of Farley's Pawn Shop. Approaching her office across the street, Dr. Jocelyn Gold shivered in the cool January air, remembering the same scene only five days before—when Earl Farley had been found dead, an apparent suicide, in his office right below his apartment on the second floor.

Was the sheriff's department completing its investigation into Earl's death? Sheriff Bradford Reed hadn't been very supportive when Earl had died, but then the Farleys didn't belong to the elite of Loomis. After the deputy left, she'd called Leah, Earl's wife, to offer to come over if she needed someone to talk to.

Jocelyn pushed her office door open and entered, hoping everything was all right with Leah, who had instantly renewed their friendship from high school when Jocelyn had returned to town nine months ago. She quickly crossed to the window and opened the blinds to allow sunlight to pour into the room. After being gone for two days to speak at a conference in New Orleans on counseling children who were victims of crime, the musty smell of a closed office accosted her.

The blinking light on her phone drew her attention. When she played her messages, Leah's voice blared from the speaker.

"Jocelyn, I need to see you. I've made a mess of everything. I'll catch you when you get back tomorrow."

Her neighbor's frantic tone heightened Jocelyn's concern. She placed a call to Leah's apartment. What was going on? A new development in Earl's death?

Please, Leah, pick up.

On the fifth ring, a gruff-sounding man answered with "Hello."

The rough voice snatched any words from Jocelyn's mind for a few seconds.

"Who's this?" the man demanded.

She tightened her hand around the receiver. "Dr. Jocelyn Gold," she said with as much authority as she could muster.

"Sheriff Reed. Why are you calling, Dr. Gold?"

"Leah's a friend. What happened? Is she alright?"

"We don't know. She's disappeared."

Jocelyn jerked up straight. "Disappeared? When? I saw her on Friday right before I left." Her friend had urged her to go and speak at the conference, saying she had Shelby and Clint to support her while Jocelyn was gone a few days.

"She's been gone hardly a day."

"Foul play?"

"Don't know. Her brother seems to think so."

Jocelyn instantly thought of Leah's three-year-old daughter. "Where's Sarah?"

"Clint Herald has her."

Leah's brother had her daughter. Relief trembled through Jocelyn. "You might want to come listen to my recorder. She left me a message. She sounded frightened."

"You're at your office?"

"Jocelyn sagged back against her oak desk, all energy draining from her. "Yes. I'll be here catching up on some paperwork."

"I'll stop by after I've finished up here."

Even after the sheriff hung up, Jocelyn held the phone to her ear for a few extra seconds. *Where's Leah? Is she okay? Does this have something to do with Earl taking his own life?*

In spite of Leah's urging, I shouldn't have gone. If I had been here, maybe she wouldn't be missing. I let her down.

She'd come back to Loomis to get away from crime. When she'd worked with the New Orleans police as a consultant dealing with traumatized children, the stress had made her long for a more laid-back place to live and a job in which she wasn't bombarded constantly with the horrors people could do to children.

Memories she refused to think about intruded her with the suddenness of a summer thunderstorm sweeping in from the Gulf of Mexico. She couldn't hold them at bay. Legs quivering, she slid down the front of the desk to the hardwood floor.

I let someone else down and he died. Please don't let it be happening again. A tear slipped from one eye and rolled down her cheek. She swiped it away, determined not to revisit her past. But the images of the lost child—and of her friend Leah—haunted her.

ONE

Several hours later, Jocelyn dropped her pen, her hand aching from writing up her clients' notes in their files. Glancing toward the window, she saw the patrol car still in front of the pawnshop. She stood, stretching her arms above her herself and rolling her head to ease the tension in her neck.

A knock sounded, and sent her whirling around toward the door. She stared at it, not moving an inch. This time someone pounded against the wood, prodding her forward. She hurried from her office into the reception area and peered out the peephole. The sight of Sam Pierce stunned her. She hadn't seen him in months—not since she'd worked that child kidnapping in New Orleans with him. It hadn't ended well, and they hadn't parted on good terms.

Sam pivoted to leave. Jocelyn quickly unlatched the lock and pulled the door open.

Halting, the over-six-foot FBI agent glanced back at her. Dressed in a black suit with a red tie, dark hair cut short, he fixed her with his intense start, his tanned features making a mockery of the cool January weather.

"Jocelyn, it's good to see you again."

The formality in his voice made her wonder if he was only trying to be polite.

"I'd like to have a word with you. Sheriff Reed said that Leah Farley left a message on your answering machine. I'd like to listen to it."

"The FBI is working Leah's disappearance?"

"Yes." He took a step forward, forcing her to move to the side to allow him into the office.

"Really. I got the impression from the sheriff he didn't think Leah had met with foul play. I'm surprised he requested your assistance."

"The mayor did. I don't believe the sheriff was too happy, but he's cooperating."

"Good, because I don't think Leah would run away and leave her daughter behind. She adored her."

"So you knew her well? Professionally or personally?" He wore a no-nonsense expression, as if they hadn't dated for four months right before she had moved to Loomis. As if he hadn't saved her life once.

Jocelyn waved Sam toward the chair in front of her desk in her office. She sat in her own chair behind it, biding her time while she gathered her composure. As a psychologist, she learned to suppress any emotions she might experience in order to deal with a client's problem. Sam's presence strained that skill.

"Personally. We're neighbors." She knew she was stating the obvious, but Sam's intense stare unnerved her, as though he remembered their time together but not fondly. He was one of the reasons she had come to Loomis nine months ago to open a private practice and teach a few classes at Loomis College.

Grinning, Sam threw a glance at the pawnshop across the street and said in a teasing tone, "Yes, I can see." Then, as though he realized he'd slipped too quickly into a casual friend-liness toward her, he stiffened, the smile gone.

His sudden change pricked her curiosity. He didn't like this any more than she did. That realization made getting through the interview a little easier. She relaxed the tensed set of her shoulders.

When she had started seeing Sam in New Orleans, she had known it wasn't wise to date someone she had to work with from time to time in volatile, intense situations. Being a con-sultant on kidnapping cases in which children were involved had thrown them together over the course of the year he'd been in the Big Easy.

Jocelyn gripped the edge of her desk. "Look, I'm happy to let you hear the recording and I'll help in any other way I can, but I insist on us putting our former relationship in the past where it belongs." The relationship started when Sam rescued her from a patient's father who tried to kill her, and it fell apart when they worked together on a kidnapping case that ended violently. Brutality had surrounded her in New Orleans. She thought she'd escaped it by coming to Loomis.

"Do you mean it? You'll help with this case? Because I was thinking we need someone with your experience." His frosty gaze melted a few degrees.

Although she now worked with all age groups, in missing-persons cases she'd only dealt with the children involved. "Well, yes. I'll help. But since children are my specialty, I'm not sure how…" She drew in a deep breath, realizing what he was asking. "Sarah. You want me to work with Leah's daughter?"

REQUEST YOUR FREE BOOKS!

2 FREE RIVETING INSPIRATIONAL NOVELS
PLUS 2 FREE MYSTERY GIFTS

YES! Please send me 2 FREE Love Inspired® Suspense novels and my 2 FREE mystery gifts (gifts are worth about $10). After receiving them, if I don't wish to receive any more books, I can return the shipping statement marked "cancel". If I don't cancel, I will receive 4 brand-new novels every month and be billed just $4.24 per book in the U.S. or $4.74 per book in Canada, plus 25¢ shipping and handling per book and applicable taxes, if any*. That's a savings of over 20% off the cover price! I understand that accepting the 2 free books and gifts places me under no obligation to buy anything. I can always return a shipment and cancel at any time. Even if I never buy another book, the two free books and gifts are mine to keep forever.

123 IDN ERXX   323 IDN ERXM

Name	(PLEASE PRINT)	
Address		Apt. #
City	State/Prov.	Zip/Postal Code

Signature (if under 18, a parent or guardian must sign)

Order online at www.LoveInspiredSuspense.com
Or mail to Steeple Hill Reader Service:

IN U.S.A.: P.O. Box 1867, Buffalo, NY 14240-1867
IN CANADA: P.O. Box 609, Fort Erie, Ontario L2A 5X3

Not valid to current subscribers of Love Inspired Suspense books.

Want to try two free books from another series?
Call 1-800-873-8635 or visit www.morefreebooks.com

* Terms and prices subject to change without notice. N.Y. residents add applicable sales tax. Canadian residents will be charged applicable provincial taxes and GST. Offer not valid in Quebec. This offer is limited to one order per household. All orders subject to approval. Credit or debit balances in a customer's account(s) may be offset by any other outstanding balance owed by or to the customer. Please allow 4 to 6 weeks for delivery. Offer available while quantities last.

Your Privacy: Steeple Hill Books is committed to protecting your privacy. Our Privacy Policy is available online at www.SteepleHill.com or upon request from the Reader Service. From time to time we make our lists of customers available to reputable third parties who may have a product or service of interest to you. If you would prefer we not share your name and address, please check here. ☐

LISUS08R

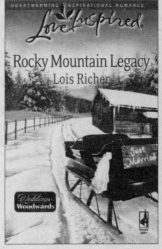

Love Inspired® SUSPENSE

TITLES AVAILABLE NEXT MONTH

Don't miss these four stories in January

HEART OF THE NIGHT by Lenora Worth
When secret agent Eli Trudeau discovers his son is alive, he's furious with Gena Malone, the boy's adoptive mother. Yet even his anger can't blind him to Gena's love for the boy. And when someone dangerous comes after them, Eli will do *anything* to protect his newfound family.

WHAT SARAH SAW by Margaret Daley
Without a Trace

The three-year-old witness is FBI agent Sam Pierce's best resource when the girl's mother vanishes. Yet child psychologist Jocelyn Gold will barely let him near Sarah. Or herself. But for the child's sake—and her mother's—Sam and Jocelyn must join forces to uncover just what Sarah saw.

BAYOU BETRAYAL by Robin Caroll
Monique Harris has found her father—in prison for murder. Still, when Monique is suddenly widowed, she seeks refuge in the bayou town of Lagniappe, not knowing *someone* doesn't want her to stay. Deputy sheriff Gary Anderson has Monique hoping for a new future... if she can lay the past to rest.

FLASHOVER by Dana Mentink
Firefighter Ivy Beria is frustrated when she's injured on the job...until she realizes the fire was no accident. The danger builds when her neighbor disappears. With the help of friend and colleague Tim Carnelli, Ivy starts searching for answers, but she might find something more—like love.

LISCNM1208BPA